GRIM TALES

AUTHORS ACROSS ENGLAND

Edited by Sarah Washer

First published in Great Britain in 2016 by:

 Young**Writers**

Remus House
Coltsfoot Drive
Peterborough
PE2 9BF
Telephone: 01733 890066
Website: www.youngwriters.co.uk

Printed and bound in the UK by BookPrintingUK
Website: www.bookprintinguk.com

FOREWORD

Welcome, Reader!

For Young Writers' latest competition, Grim Tales, we gave secondary school pupils nationwide the tricky task of writing a story with a beginning, middle and an end in just 100 words. They could either write a completely original tale or add a twist to a well-loved classic. They rose to the challenge magnificently!

We chose stories for publication based on style, expression, imagination and technical skill. The result is this entertaining collection full of diverse and imaginative mini sagas, which is also a delightful keepsake to look back on in years to come.

Here at Young Writers our aim is to encourage creativity in young adults and to inspire a love of the written word, so it's great to get such an amazing response, with some absolutely fantastic stories. This made it a tough challenge to pick the winners, so well done to Hannah Hillier who has been chosen as the best author in this anthology.

I'd like to congratulate all the young authors in Grim Tales - Authors Across England - I hope this inspires them to continue with their creative writing. And who knows, maybe we'll be seeing their names on the best seller lists in the future...

Jenni Bannister

Editorial Manager

CONTENTS

Emma Marion Peel Kilpatrick (15)............ 1
Elle Jade Suffling (13) 1
Bibi Sara Sahibzada 2
Rhys Matthews (13)................................ 2
Mason Peach (12) 3
Ichhuca Rai (11) 3
Isabelle Butcher (12) & Tia 4
Armanc Balanur (13) 4
Krish Parmar (14) 5

AYLESTONE BUSINESS & ENTERPRISE COLLEGE, HEREFORD
Shannon Dowzell (15) 5
Patrycja Panocka (14) 6
Lewis Craddock (15)............................... 6
Kieran Holland (15)................................. 7
Elliot Tindale (15)................................... 7
Charlotte Tippins (15) 8
Shania Davies-Lewis (15)........................ 8
Edita Sedoikina....................................... 9
Lawrence Hoskins (15)........................... 9
Conor McNeil (15) 10
Laura Harris (15) 10
Saffron Holland (15) 11
Jade Evans (15)....................................11
David Cani (15)..................................... 12
Phoebe Leigh Jones (15) 13
Daniel Chambers (15) 14
Zoe Mansell (15)................................... 14
Tully Jones (15)..................................... 15
Gintare Stockute (15) 15
Abbie Preece (15).................................. 16
Rees Newton-Sealey (15) 16
Molly Evans (16).................................... 17
Chloe Bendall (15)................................. 17
Kyran Hopkins (15)................................ 18
Taylor McNeil (16).................................. 18
Helen Hughes (15) 19
Rachel Bell (15)..................................... 19
Jack Tyler (15)....................................... 20
Kyle Jones (15)...................................... 20
Jordan Easdale (15) 21

Leah Jones (15)..................................... 21
Emily Olivia Boyle (15) 22
Millie James (14) 22
Ziv Omar Alvarez (15)............................ 23
Billie Hyett (16) 23
Shannon Griffiths (15) 24
Hannah May Broad (15) 24
Harvey Williams (14) 25
Namking Chocksawat (15) 25
Katherine Kan (15) 26

BARTON MOSS EDUCATION UNIT, MANCHESTER
Kyle Major (15)...................................... 26
Fred Grey (16)....................................... 27
Corey James Hewitt (15)........................ 27

BAXTER COLLEGE, KIDDERMINSTER
Jade Cassidy-Adams (15) 28
Fay Goerlach (15).................................. 28
Olivia Atherton (13)............................... 29
Daniel Correia (15)................................ 29
Elinor Neville (15) 30

CARDINAL NEWMAN CATHOLIC SCHOOL - A SPECIALIST SCIENCE COLLEGE, LUTON
Kira Mclean (16) 31

HAYBRIDGE HIGH SCHOOL & SIXTH FORM, STOURBRIDGE
Cameron Pearcey (15)........................... 32
Cavan West (14)..................................... 32
Emily Ann Mae Dennis (14)..................... 33
Eva Gray (15).. 33
Felix Farrow (15) 34
Grace Clifford (15) 34
Jenny Kendall (15)................................. 35
Kia Starks (14)...................................... 35
Lucy Robson (15) 36
Maddie Baker (15)................................. 36

Maisie Rawle (15)...................................... 37
Rose Winn (15)... 37

HOPE ACADEMY, NEWTON-LE-WILLOWS

Ella Sophie Tomlinson (12)...................... 38
Grace Amelia Burnett (12)....................... 38
Thomas Harry Bennett (12).................... 39
Chloe Nicole Brenda Frayne (12)........... 39
Sajidah Rahman (12).............................. 40
Sam Fagan.. 40
Lucy O'Reilly (14) 41
Daniel Philip Richards (14)..................... 41
Tom Steven Burnett (12)......................... 42
Ellie Shard (12)....................................... 43
Leah Blinstone (12) 44
Keira Louise Blood (12)........................... 44
Alex Hayden (12)..................................... 45
Megan Louise Thorpe (13) 45
Leslie Calvin Kara (13) 46
Shannon Smith (13)................................ 46
Aolani Louise Kinsey (13)....................... 47
Brandon Stokes (12).............................. 47
Rebecca Heaton (13) 48
Phoebe Chandler (13) 48
Matthew Edwards (13)............................ 49
Liam Lupton.. 49
Chloe Whiteley (13)................................ 50
Joe Abernethy (12)................................. 50
Nathan Bevan (12) 51
Joseph Thomas Robert Charleston (12) 51
Bradley Harrison (12) 52
Chloe Hooper (12).................................. 52
Gabrielle Rose Barnes (12).................... 53
Daniel Hill (13)....................................... 53
Ross Anthony Booth (13)........................ 54
Alex Skeech (13) 54

JOHN MASEFIELD HIGH SCHOOL, LEDBURY

Poppy Park... 55
Amy Hill 55

KENILWORTH SCHOOL & SPORTS COLLEGE, KENILWORTH

Joseph Bartholomew.............................. 56
Jeevan Singh Virdi (13) 56

Tia Rose Eales (15)................................ 57
Zaynab Iqbal (12) 57
Onkar Matharu (14)................................ 58
Amy Goodwin (14).................................. 58
Hannah Matthews (14) 59
Amy Hall (14).. 59
Henry Maggs (14)................................... 60
Enrico Bucci (14) 60
Jodie Ward (14)...................................... 61
Lulabelle Thomas-Manuel (14)............... 61
Charlie May Nicholls (13) 62
Holly Coop (12)....................................... 62
Zoe Wilkinson (13).................................. 63
Isabelle Dorrington (13).......................... 63
Charlie Simcox (13)................................ 64
Aaron Whitehouse Pope (14) 64
Lucy Woodward (13) 65
Jessica Peck (14) 65
Joshua Daniel Hardy Butler (14) 66
Katie May Stockbridge (14).................... 67
Louis Perry (14)...................................... 68
Megan Heath (14)................................... 68
Alexandra Scott (14)............................... 69
Alexander Darlow (14)............................ 69
Isabelle Perry (13).................................. 70
Erin Myles (13) 70
Keeley Davis (13)................................... 71
Katie Coulter (13) 71
Elise Herrington..................................... 72
Iona Ward (12).. 72
Jordan Howes... 73

MANCHESTER HEALTH ACADEMY, MANCHESTER

Joseph Green (12).................................. 73
Taylor Hickford....................................... 74
Hannah Bindon (14) 74
Emily Matthews (14)............................... 75
Lauren Fielding (14) 75
Hannah Bentham (14) 76
Kate Wilson (14)..................................... 76
Nicol Rad (12)... 77

MEADOWHEAD SCHOOL, SHEFFIELD

Harry Wooldridge.................................... 77

Rainsbrook Secure Training Centre, Rugby

Josh Aisthorpe (17)............................... 78
Alex Smith (16)...................................... 78

St Bernard's Catholic High School, Barrow-in-Furness

Jamie Baker (11) 79
Scarlett Kenny (11)................................ 79
Lucas Kay (12) 80
Charlotte North (11)................................ 80
Joseph Thompson (13)........................... 81
Bethany Hewson (11) 81
Varenka Briggs (11) 82

Stratford-upon-Avon School, Stratford-upon-Avon

Lauren Jeffries (15) 82
Hana Adler (15) 83
Holly Sumners (15)................................ 83
Freya Stiff (16).. 84
Jazmin Lea Cartwright (14) 85
Freya Barnett (14) 86
Lewis Noble (12)..................................... 86
Lily McMeekan (15)................................ 87
Daniel Godefroy (14) 87
Olivia Joan Bailey (12)........................... 88
Ruby Wade (12) 88
Kiera Kennedy (11)................................ 89
Thalie Coleta-Sibley (12)....................... 89
Molly Rose Flanagan (12) 90
Hannah Jeffs (11) 90
Louis Sobral-Kilmister (12) 91
Daniel Malone (15) 91
Mathilda Ward (12)................................. 92
Ellie Rose Marshall (12) 92
Ella Wilson (12) 93
Georgie Burton (12)................................ 93
Nadia-Jane Rogers (12) 94
Joshua Stephens (12) 94
Edie Clarke (12)...................................... 95
Hannah Hillier (15)................................. 95
William Jones (12)................................... 96
Bethany Caitlin Harris (15) 96

Ullswater Community College, Penrith

Teri Ann Chadwick (12)........................... 97
Gabrielle Jane Bailey (12) 97
Davina Louise Ivinson McAneney (12)... 98
Lauren Hannah Clarke (12)................... 98
Evie Farndon (12)................................... 99
Rosie Elizabeth Dale (12)...................... 99
Freya Colling (12)................................. 100
Daniel Bennett (12)............................... 100
Layla Threlkeld (12).............................. 101
Samuel Potts (12)................................. 101
Emily Law (12)...................................... 102
Lily Webb (11)....................................... 102
Edward Spence (12).............................. 103
Jake Stamper (12)................................ 103
Ellie Howard (12).................................. 104
Katie Jackson (12)................................ 104
Macy Ella Hicks (12)............................. 105
Naomi Harris (12) 105
Jamie Cowperthwaite (11)................... 106
Beah Lamis (12) 107
Charlotte Carrick (12) 108
Chloe Dalton (13) 108
Molly Ella Kirkman (12)........................ 109
Shannon Southward (12)...................... 109
Robert Hopkinson (11)...........................110
Isabella Grace Nattrass (12).................110
Alex Huddart (12) 111
Niamh Brenan (11) 111
Savannah Edwards-Lynch (12) 112
Saskia Todd (12)....................................112
Charlie Kirkland (12).............................113

William Howard School, Brampton

Kelina May Marshall (14)........................113
Charlotte Hetherington (14)...................114
Lewis Logie (14) 114
Emily Garson (14)..................................115

The
Mini Sagas

THE LOST SOUL

As the rusty chain arm breaks off and clatters to the floor, dead silence falls in the large empty warehouse. Stumbling around, searching for his soul, he's nothing without it. The large thuds of his heavy metal feet hitting the ground, trying hard to put one foot in front of the other. Sensing his soul is somewhere near he struggles on with mighty determination. The sensation of feeling human again, able to do normal things, not being chased and called a monster is all he wants. His soul back. His normal life back. The key to his soul is near.

EMMA MARION PEEL KILPATRICK (15)

THE MYSTERY GIRL

On a dark and gloomy night, she was slowly walking in the pitch-black in a forest. A man came up to her and put his hands around her neck. Police had been looking for this girl for ages. No one knew her name, her age or anything about her. She was a mystery. The reason people were looking for her was because she had murdered children. As the man's hands got tighter and tighter she turned around and screamed as loud as she could. She reached in her pocket, took out her knife and the man had his last breath.

ELLE JADE SUFFLING (13)

BLOOD BANK

With a few mighty bounds, they captured me, digging their claws into my skin. The agonising pain grew as the beasts surrounded! The excruciating pain! The unendurable ache became heavier as they started shredding me. I was lost in a sea of blood that belonged to me as they snarled in victory. I felt light-headed and vertiginous from the extreme pain. My vision became nebulous... the cacophony silenced.
Pain... gone.
I looked at my fingers, ashen and ghastly, I reached for the ashes. Unable to feel, unable to touch. The reality dawned on me as dark clouds shifted...
I'd died.

BIBI SARA SAHIBZADA

THE ZOMBIE APOCALYPSE

It was a zombie apocalypse. My best friend Victor and I, were forced from our homes and were stranded on a big farm with one old wooden house. There was one small problem, there were zombies everywhere surrounding the place. All I had on me was a bow with four arrows, so did Victor, he also had an axe. The zombies looked very ugly with their green eyes, blood dripping down their faces. There were seven of these nasty things about. We killed them all. We arrived in the house and found a brilliant machine gun but Victor was dead.

RHYS MATTHEWS (13)

REMEMBER

Little Blue lived in a cottage in the woods. She was adventurous and loved to explore.
One day, she went into the woods to look for a new ingredient for her cake. She stumbled upon an old house, she went inside. She saw a boy sitting on a wooden stool… when he turned around. 'Remember me?' he whispered. The boy looked badly burned. When he got up, he walked towards her, doors shut; as he approached, Little Blue felt cold, she saw hands at her throat. 'Remember,' he said.
She woke up at her brother's grave… 'I remember Louis.'

MASON PEACH (12)

MEMORIES

The night crept in, every move that was made changed the atmosphere. Loud thuds could be heard from the hall. Memories flashed back all at one time, unwanted. How she missed those days when laughter echoed through the walls. Mrs Eve missed that so much. Now all that was left was a house filled with silence. Every day started and ended in complete silence. She'd been deprived of her love at the age of 78. She was already in her eighties. Now she felt as it it was her time to go. She knew why and what memories were for.

ICHHUCA RAI (11)

Red Eyes And Fred

I was walking at the other end, its red eyes were staring, a black figure was there… It was approaching me quicker, quicker my heart was pumping. I was walking towards it then it stopped and turned away. I ran to it but it ran away so I got quicker until we got to the outskirts of the forest. It turned and growled then, all of a sudden, it jumped straight at me. It bit my arm, leaving me bleeding. I thought I was going to die… I woke still lying there. I walked home into my bed, dying painfully.

Isabelle Butcher (12) & Tia

Racing Online With My Friends

'Come on, only five left to overtake,' I sped past the 5th and the 4th car. I started to gain even more speed. Then I caught up with the Ferrari 458 Spider, which Nearle was driving; passed him with a drift and then his car's engine burst. Now catching up with Dillon, driving the Ferrari LaFerrari. 'Passed!' 2nd place trying to catch Dongda with his Lamborghini Veneno. As I passed him, I shouted, 'Ohh!' So close to the finish line, but *bang!* My car engine died. 'Nooo, how could this happen?'

Armanc Balanur (13)

THE SEEKER

Homeless came running... and running through the darkness among the gusty trees, closer and closer, shouting, 'Help!' in an empty, isolated road. Eventually, he heard a skateboard coming like a stream of lava from Devils Fall cave. He looked nervously over his shoulder, terrified, thinking nothing was there. He saw! He saw him... He saw him coming closer and closer in the gusty galleon white sea of cloudy night, shouting, 'Is there anybody there?' He saw him again! He saw the enormous man with a mask of the Joker. He came down through the road with a blooded axe!

KRISH PARMAR (14)

REVENGE!

Sadness fills my eyes. He's dead! Ursula killed my last piece of happiness. Was cutting my tail not enough? One kiss, that's all it took for him to disappear. Trembling, watching Ursula's revolting smirk whilst piercing, striking Eric's remains. Emptiness surrounds, suffocating me. Slowly her back turned away, leaving me with the painted blade. *Now it's your turn!* Bit by bit I punctured. Blood pouring, splattering everywhere. Revenge is a plate best served cold. Pungent odour expands the air. The scraps of Ursula's body within her own fusty filth, nothing was left now. Eric was gone, it was too late!

SHANNON DOWZELL (15)
Aylestone Business & Enterprise College, Hereford

Blood And Chains

I fearfully wandered up the stairs. Not knowing where they led. I heard voices telling me to stop, but I didn't listen. I kept wandering. She was there, looking wonderful. Black hair, pale skin, smiling at me with stitches in her mouth. I looked down. Gushing down her neck - blood. She's coming close to me. She stopped. Are those chains? With spikes? I stepped back. Her eyes pure black, smiling at me. She screamed. Everything went pitch-black. Blood was everywhere, pouring down the walls, blood, just blood. Close to my face. She smiled. It was black, just black…

Patrycja Panocka (14)
Aylestone Business & Enterprise College, Hereford

Charlie And The Chocolate Factory

Augustus Gloop was a very peckish boy. He bathed Charlie's head in chocolate sauce, tore his head off with his teeth and sucked his guts out and spat them out! After that, he clutched Charlie's feet and bit his toes off one by one. His next victim - Willy Wonka! Suddenly he swiped for him. He volleyed Wonka's head into the sauce. Augustus picked up what was left of Wonka then devoured him. Abruptly Augustus fell to the floor. He had been shot. His mother cried. It was the end for Augustus.

Lewis Craddock (15)
Aylestone Business & Enterprise College, Hereford

THE PLIGHT AGAINST EVIL

Knock, knock, knock. The door opens. There's no one there. I whistle. Yet the birds don't come. I know that any day may be my last: by death. They came for me, still I must work. They will come. On their horses march many, the seven sinners. My only hope lay in the hands of solely one… the evil queen. Only the evillest can defeat evil. The clock strikes seven. Three hours till my fate is sealed… *Knock! Knock! Knock!* Who lurks outside? The door opens… My destiny has been fulfilled. The clock strikes ten. The sun has set.

KIERAN HOLLAND (15)
Aylestone Business & Enterprise College, Hereford

CHARLIE AND THE CHOCOLATE FACTORY

Whilst Willy was helping everyone onto the oversized boat. Augustus was desiring food; even though he had a family-sized chocolate bar in his right hand and a double scoop ice cream clenched in his left. Finally, it was time for Augustus to board. Willie was hesitant, the boat tilted. Wonka thought it would be alright. Whilst travelling, the boat tipped so far that everyone had to hold on. Augustus took his chance. Suddenly, he stood and sat down with force. Gloop opened his gaping mouth, everyone tumbled into his mouth. He clamped down. The Oompa-Loompas scarpered!

ELLIOT TINDALE (15)
Aylestone Business & Enterprise College, Hereford

Rapunzel, Let Down Your Hair

Leaving the rotting tower, he realised he had made a huge mistake. He turned back. He commanded Rapunzel let down her hair. There was no reply. Worried, he called again. Still no reply until suddenly blood poured from the shattered window. He paced rapidly up the stairs. Blood was everywhere. A trickling noise came from behind him. He turned, the wardrobe opened and there Rapunzel hung. Pale as a ghost. Her wrists had been sliced open. Lurking in the shadows was a mysterious killer who sprinted down the stairs and into the distance.

CHARLOTTE TIPPINS (15)
Aylestone Business & Enterprise College, Hereford

The Captain

Chains and shackles scraped along the rotting decks. Blood dripped down into the cabins underneath. It splattered onto the sleeping crew. Peter and Wendy were chained to the mast, buckets of cannonballs either side attached the chains. Tearing their arms out of their sockets, blood splattered from limbs, splashed onto their stretched bodies. A putrid smell of ripped flesh filled their nostrils with terror. Then the wooden staircase creaked. Their hearts sank when they saw him. They called him Captain. He towered above everyone, sneering down into their petrified eyes.

SHANIA DAVIES-LEWIS (15)
Aylestone Business & Enterprise College, Hereford

THE HARMLESS YOUNG SNOW WHITE

The innocent, pale, round face with bright red lips lay frozen in a glass coffin. Whilst the seventh dwarf appeared from behind the coffin, shivering in suspicion, the last six surrounded him; they only had minutes until the death and White would lay still forever. The dwarfs hastily held a weapon of fear and blood, that would touch the young girl through her loneliness, young heart dripping its last tear. From far away, the disgraceful madam reappeared: the evil queen. The moment the queen shattered the door, Snow White unsealed her eyes, knowing it was her privilege to live…

EDITA SEDOIKINA
Aylestone Business & Enterprise College, Hereford

PETER PAN, THE HERO

Suddenly, I felt the ship sinking. I could not do anything, because there was no help. I just stared at my boat. I was shocked. When the boat sank, I fell into the sea. Sharks lurked menacingly. I was terrified. Peter Pan rescued me while Captain Hook swam to shore with all of his treasure in his pockets. Peter Pan was watching him. Captain Hook had seen Peter Pan. Peter Pan had an idea, he would kidnap Captain Hook or rob him.
Peter Pan made his move. The fight started. Swords were banging...

LAWRENCE HOSKINS (15)
Aylestone Business & Enterprise College, Hereford

PETER PAN

Trembling, Captain Hook embraced his treasure. Diamonds and gold falling into the wet abyss, Captain was crying like a baby. His life submerged in chaos. *Swoosh.* Captain vanished. Cemented to the treasure. Captain was mugged. Peter Pan whittled disgrace across Captain's hairy chest. Blood filled the lagoon with scarlet ruby water. The Lost Boys powered through the steel prison. Blood pouring from their shattered knuckles. Monstrosities. Scared faces and blood dripping from their mouths. Blood squirted from the stump of the captain's neck. Peter plummeted to his treasure. Ten daggers contrived Peter Pan's black heart. Peter disintegrated…

CONOR MCNEIL (15)
Aylestone Business & Enterprise College, Hereford

UNTITLED

With her knife at the ready, she hurried down the corridor. Heading towards her stepmother's room, she mutely strode in. Taking ninja-like steps towards her, the knife raised above her head, swooping back and forth to the sound of her breathing. The sound of screams echoed followed by silence. The innocent-looking girl grinned at the sight of her witch of a mum lying silently on the floor.

LAURA HARRIS (15)
Aylestone Business & Enterprise College, Hereford

THE END OF BEAUTY

There. A brunette innocently laid. The beast sniffed. Red roses.
His eyes snapped to hers. Fear. She was scared of him; he was
intimidating. His teeth were bared and nails sharp. The chain, melted
to her legs, burned. Her hair, like straw, was standing tall. A single,
salty tear marched down her porcelain face. Her crimson cuts stood
out against the plain background. She was a beauty. The beast
advanced…

SAFFRON HOLLAND (15)
Aylestone Business & Enterprise College, Hereford

THE REAL TALE OF SNOW WHITE

Gazing into her misty mirror she knew her plan was ready for action.
She would hunt down poor Snow White. Running through the forest
with her flowing black cape. The dwarfs were in on the plan, taking
her to the centre of the forest at noon. It was time, Snow White was
there. Out ran evil Stepmum with revenge and malicious murder in
her eyes. However, Snow White already lay there dead! With an evil
cackle she handed over a case full of money as a reward for the
dwarfs' impeccable murder.

JADE EVANS (15)
Aylestone Business & Enterprise College, Hereford

Sleeping Beauty's Tale Awakens

Licking his lips, he strolled towards the bed. His mind was a spectrum of possibilities as he finally approached. There she lay, Sleeping Beauty; unable to hear or awaken due to the wretched thorn. He, Prince Charming, looked at her body with mysterious delight and wiped his hands. He struggled as he reached his shivering hand but pulled back… He took a deep, shivery breath. Charming's hands made their way onto her dress. His mind was rushing, his fear of her awakening wisely grew. He moved his hands away which left sweat stains, leant over towards her face, she awakened…

David Cani (15)
Aylestone Business & Enterprise College, Hereford

Little Red Riding Horror

Her rumbling tummy could only be satisfied by one thing. Wolf! Her eyes skimmed the forest in hope of finding the meal of her dreams. There he was, she knew there was only one thing to do! As she danced over to her feast, a big, devilish grin appeared on her chubby, baby face. Skipping away, she knew he would follow her. They always did!

Finally, they both arrived at her humble home, she welcomed him with open arms; well… she would do! All went silent! Slowly but surely she turned around and muttered the words, 'It's feeding time.' 'Argh!'

Phoebe Leigh Jones (15)
Aylestone Business & Enterprise College, Hereford

13

THE FALLING GIRL

I walked through the awoken forest, I came to a tower lurking high above the clouds. My natural instinct was to climb so I did. I was dodging rocks and stones as I got higher and higher. I leaned through the so-called window. Darkness filled the room. Then suddenly a gust of wind slammed open a cupboard. Gold everywhere. All of it mine for the taking. I turned around to see a figure blocking the light, she had blonde glistening hair, I only like brunettes. With one mighty kick she went flying out the window. Time to go…

DANIEL CHAMBERS (15)
Aylestone Business & Enterprise College, Hereford

UNTITLED

My heart was beating so fast, I didn't know what to do. I stood facing the beast with my back flat against the wall, with a look of determination on his face. I took long deep breaths thinking they could be my last. He took one last step closer to me, stamping his paws hard into the ground. He started to dribble. I could tell what was going through his mind but luckily he couldn't tell what was going through mine. Out of the corner of my eye, I noticed a sharp blade. With one sharp swing, he was gone.

ZOE MANSELL (15)
Aylestone Business & Enterprise College, Hereford

GANDALF IN WONDERLAND?

He woke with a start. The grey garbed wizard inhaled deeply as the screams of innocent children and women were projected across the city. Instantaneously, he was striding along the cobbled road, walking between rows of houses crumbling under intense flames. His gaze transfixed upon a single individual, laughing while gesturing to the burning flames. The Mad Hatter's smile nearly intimidating the old man, the duel was swift. Gandalf quickly parried a strong blow and RKO'd the Hatter out of nowhere. It was, however, short-lived. As Shrek ran from behind a house and 420 blazed them both.

TULLY JONES (15)
Aylestone Business & Enterprise College, Hereford

SNOW WHITE'S REVENGE

She was running through the woods, trying to escape her evil clutches. Running to the place where no one could find her, escaping from the evil queen, she wanted to be the fairest, she needed her revenge. Snow White went to the mirror, where her stepmother sat looking at her beauty. Snow White suddenly smashed the mirror and shards of glass flew at the queen's face. She let out a hideous shriek. The mirror had captured her beauty forever. Snow White laughed, her revenge was complete.

GINTARE STOCKUTE (15)
Aylestone Business & Enterprise College, Hereford

UNDER THE COVERS

Howling winds ripped leaves from trees, ammunition in the brutal gale. A knock. Ushered through the door, her prince awaited her. Yawning, the princess shrugged off her cloak and gazed at the bed of mattresses before her. A prick on her finger, a strange lump under the cover. Trembling hands lifted duvets, revealing the sharp blade. She grasped the knife, turned to the old lady at the door. A low gasp, a flick of the wrist and a rotting corpse in the gutter. A trail of blood, a guttural moan and the prince was dead. Happily ever after for her.

ABBIE PREECE (15)
Aylestone Business & Enterprise College, Hereford

THE DEADLY ARROW

Robin Hood. A name feared throughout the land. The mere sight of his bow struck terror into the hearts of peasants, his quiver a deathly black. In the past few days, multiple people had fallen to his fatal arrows. However, this was not due to ruthlessness. It was simply because his archery skills were horrendous. One day, he made the worst shot in his life. The arrow curved mid-air, returning to its source like a boomerang. The arrow entered his eye, spewing red sticky brain fluid onto the field behind him. The town was finally safe from Robin Hood.

REES NEWTON-SEALEY (15)
Aylestone Business & Enterprise College, Hereford

CINDER'S REVENGE

This was her chance. Revenge would be hers. The beloved, wrinkled Prince Charming would die on this eve. Cinder's father would be avenged.
In the ballroom, Cinder's unsheathed the golden knife and impaled it into his chest. Death is glory. A sharp pain seared through her back. Cinder's stumbled then collapsed to the floor. Blood pooled throughout the ballroom. Insane grins came across the ugly sisters' marred faces. Maybe revenge isn't so sweet!

MOLLY EVANS (16)
Aylestone Business & Enterprise College, Hereford

THE REVENGE OF CINDERELLA

Revenge. She will have her revenge. Cinders trailed behind her sisters to the ball, but they would not return. Arriving, she plunged her weapon into everyone, but one man. Prince Charming! The deed completed. She escaped, but she lost one thing. The killer. The knife. The only survivor collected her knife. One scream, joined with a thud. The prince forced agonising pain through her back. One stab and she was dead. But who eventually got their revenge?

CHLOE BENDALL (15)
Aylestone Business & Enterprise College, Hereford

CINDERELLA AND HER UGLY SISTERS

Cinderella was in her room when the prince called round with the golden slipper located in his hand. Her ugly stepsisters boisterously pushed her out the way and said they were the ones who wore the lovely slipper. Cinderella retaliated, grabbed a machete and sliced their feet off! Then left their corpses to bleed to death. She then trampled over their lifeless bodies before linking arms with her prince to ride off into the sunset. Their dreams were fulfilled.

KYRAN HOPKINS (15)
Aylestone Business & Enterprise College, Hereford

THE PRINCE AND THE DUNGEON

My dungeon was really horrible, disgusting. I literally couldn't remember how I'd ended up in this place, but, whoever did this was certainly going to pay. I was looking out of my cell window thinking how I was going to get out of here. Did anyone know I was in here? Did anyone care? I heard thumps out of the dungeon. I called, 'Hello?' Still no reply. But out of nowhere, there was the most beautiful girl I'd ever seen in my entire life. She came to save me!

TAYLOR MCNEIL (16)
Aylestone Business & Enterprise College, Hereford

GUNS AND GOWNS

Life seemed so surreal. First, the fairy godmother and now this ball… I turned to see the prince. As he glanced up, our eyes connected. *Bang!* Screams of terror erupted. A group of men burst in. 'Give us the girl!' I fell to my knees after being shoved from behind. The leader yanked me forward by my hair, tears filled my eyes. I had no time to feel anything except the cold barrel of a gun pressed against my head. *Bang!* I sat up with a gasp. I heard my brother's shooting game stop.
'Turn your stupid princess film down!'

HELEN HUGHES (15)
Aylestone Business & Enterprise College, Hereford

SLEEPING BEAUTY'S SAVIOUR

Dark. Isolated. Asleep. Sleeping Beauty lay on a bed of solitude; his eyes locked shut. The rectangle light of the window darkened. Someone was coming in. They strode over to the bed and with a slap, he awoke suddenly. Who had saved him? A knight? No, a girl. Leather jackets replaced silver armour. Crossbows replaced swords. 'Wakey, wakey, Sleeping Beauty,' she calmly spoke. 'You must be confused. All I'll say is welcome to the apocalypse.' He turned the door, harrowing groans echoed. Zombies. That was the last time he drank before bed.

RACHEL BELL (15)
Aylestone Business & Enterprise College, Hereford

THE WICKED WOODSMAN!

(Carrying on from the original story)… Red Riding Hood arrived at her grandma's house. The door was broken down and the inside ransacked. She walked in. Through the rubble. Her grandma was nowhere to be found. Suddenly, a scream of distress sounded from the forest outside. At the noise she turned to see a note stuck to the wall by an axe: 'If you want to see your grandma again, bring the wolf to the cabin deep in the woods', signed by the woodsman. She walked out with a blank expression on her face. The wolf knew, and he was waiting.

JACK TYLER (15)
Aylestone Business & Enterprise College, Hereford

UNTITLED

The three bears were preparing their trap. Cooking a delicious, teasing bowl of porridge, placed in the window drawing Goldie in. Goldie took a big sniff, smelling the porridge. She slowly lifted the spoon to her lips and swallowed. It slowly slipped down her throat. Poison. She dropped to the ground like a rag doll. The bears grinned, as they emerged from their hiding places. Chuckling they lifted her body and placed it in the roasting tray. Yum! Yum!

KYLE JONES (15)
Aylestone Business & Enterprise College, Hereford

HEROIC HEART

An attractive princess, in a blood-soaked castle. Ironic isn't it? What she chose? Her saviour - the doctor. She had assumed a false identity. A disturbed princess. Belonging in Hell, Hell alone. She swooped down to a dying, lonely boy. Smirking, she stabbed him, feeling his final heartbeat. A screech alerted her to its presence, her dragon, eyes of fire, breath of death. It held a man, she knew his face, bloody and battered. Limbs missing, but eyes bright. Her saviour. The fire roasted his bones, smacking her lips. She tucked in, tasting his heroic heart.

JORDAN EASDALE (15)
Aylestone Business & Enterprise College, Hereford

THE DEEP, DARK WOODS

It was dark, gloomy, foggy and unpredictable. Little Red Riding Hood decided that she wanted to go on a walk… She walked and walked for miles. Little Red Riding Hood came upon a dark rancid house, there was no one to be seen. She looked through the old, rotten, worn out window; what she saw couldn't be unseen. An old lady lay on the floor, whilst a funny-looking wolf stood over her. He saw Red and ran. She smashed through the window and went to the old lady's rescue. She had already been taken. Red walked away terrified.

LEAH JONES (15)
Aylestone Business & Enterprise College, Hereford

THE DARKNESS

The clouds blanketed the kingdom, blocking every inch of light. Her blue eyes gaped open as darkness fell upon her. She was hungry for revenge. Maleficent was responsible for killing the innocent girl now lost inside of her. Muttering thought flooded her mind, Aurora's first victim was Maleficent. As Aurora rode her horse into the forest, she fell upon her prey. Maleficent looked like she had seen a ghost. As she glanced upon Aurora's eyes she saw they were now filled with evil and she knew she didn't stand a chance against the darkness that was now inside Sleeping Beauty.

EMILY OLIVIA BOYLE (15)
Aylestone Business & Enterprise College, Hereford

MURDER IN THE TOWER

It started with a girl trapped in a tower. Stones grazing his hands after every move. When he reached the top, he gazed upon her face. She was more beautiful than he imagined. He leaned in. His lips touched hers. She plunged a knife into his heart. She looked into his eyes watching his life drain away. She skipped joyfully to the window ledge. She looked down. Her victims had been consumed by overgrown grass. She stepped onto the ledge. She took one final breath. She jumped…

MILLIE JAMES (14)
Aylestone Business & Enterprise College, Hereford

SMALL HEROIC MAN

A huge lion was lost in a village. The villagers went inside their huts. A man ran quickly to Arc, asking him to kill the lion. Ben saw the lion beside his hut. Growling and searching for food. As Arc went out of his hut, the lion grabbed and bit him on his back. Ben grabbed a sword and slew it. The lion fell down. Ben felt proud of himself. The villagers gave a blessed bow and sword to Ben as his reward. Ben was the most heroic man of them all.

ZIV OMAR ALVAREZ (15)
Aylestone Business & Enterprise College, Hereford

THE HOPELESS PRINCESS

She was sat in the forest all alone in the cold. As she looked up, she saw a handsome young man. Cinderella fell in love with him straight away. She didn't care that she didn't know anything about him. They walked back to the young man's castle, but Cinderella didn't know the prince's secret.
One night, when Cinderella was sleeping, the prince snuck into Cinderella's room and whispered to her, 'Don't worry Darling, it won't hurt,' and then he pulled out a gun and shot her.

BILLIE HYETT (16)
Aylestone Business & Enterprise College, Hereford

Let Down Your Hair

She had been in that tower too long. She had forgotten what being social was and the thought of seeing another human being was overwhelming. She was weaker than ever and clumps of hair were surrounding her. She couldn't handle the intense isolation any longer and the single window seemed more enticing each day. Her emotions were towering as she approached the only exit of the prison and her fragile skin shuddered as it made contact with the rotting ledge. Standing up straight and stretching she stepped over the edge, finally free.

SHANNON GRIFFITHS (15)
Aylestone Business & Enterprise College, Hereford

Little Red Riding Hood Inside Out

A hungry girl's eyes scanned the dark, gloomy woods. She had an appetite. Her stomach only wanted one food - wolf! But first she had to get the wolf to inveigle her. She skipped towards the wolf to get him into her trap. He couldn't see it but she was smiling. The girl knew that the wolf would follow her back home; they always did… Then the young girl welcomed him into her home. As the girl was looking at the wolf (wiggling her fingers) she thought, *it's time for a snack…*

HANNAH MAY BROAD (15)
Aylestone Business & Enterprise College, Hereford

Predator Of The Beast

The snapping twigs prompted a sprint from the girl. She suspected that something was following. As she ran, her gown caught on a twig, falling into a pit. She awoke with blood gushing from her head and down her face. Then she saw it… A beast towered above her and a look of fear was on her face. The beast went for the throat. Before the beast's teeth made contact with her flesh the girl was grabbed by two men in white scrubs who injected her. Before she could react, the woods disappeared and the beast was no more.

Harvey Williams (14)
Aylestone Business & Enterprise College, Hereford

Lost The Love

A pale face and rosy-lipped girl called Snow White. Reflecting in 14 eyeballs. They stared at her maliciously. Beneath her chin they held a sharp knife. She trembled. These people hated her. The knife moved closer to her neck. Unexpectedly, the knife lingered to the youngest dwarf's heart. Silently, youngest dwarf dropped to the floor. Tears began to fall down. A girl grinned with victory. The royal stepmother had followed her order. As always! Their precious love had died. Angrily, they attacked the girl. The mother had lost her only love. Crying sounds were everywhere…

Namking Chocksawat (15)
Aylestone Business & Enterprise College, Hereford

Seeing

In the dark he glimpses a glowing hood. Red like freshly spilt blood. Skin as pale as moonlight. Hair as dark as the night. Eyes piercing blue in the dark of the night. In one hand a basket with a delicately placed blanket on top. The other hand a silver dagger stained with rusted crimson. She is watching him with these piercing eyes. He runs. She strolls. He stops. She's next to him. He howls for help. He dies. She wears his bloody skin on her crimson hood. She takes the body dripping with the life-sustaining liquid…

KATHERINE KAN (15)
Aylestone Business & Enterprise College, Hereford

Untitled

Once upon a time, I was walking through the forest and I was picking berries and then I saw a hairy tail. Then I saw some pointy ears, then I saw some big eyes and I noticed some big fangs. I started shaking and hid behind a tree. I heard the big bad wolf creeping through the long grass getting closer and closer and closer. I turned around and ran as fast as I could then I tripped up over a log and sprained my ankle. The wolf peered over me, panting. He said, 'Have you got the time mate?'

KYLE MAJOR (15)
Barton Moss Education Unit, Manchester

EDGE OF THE WORLD

Once upon a time, my dream was to go to the edge of the world. One day, a little pony told me how to get there by travelling in a spaceship. I spent months trying to get there and at last I arrived. I saw a huge stone at the edge of the world, there was lots of gold and jewels running down like it was chocolate. I saw a big friendly giant ogre. He was so nice and he let me look around his magnificent castle. He quietly handed me a small bag of colourful moving magic black beans.

FRED GREY (16)
Barton Moss Education Unit, Manchester

THE LOVELY DINNER

The three bears lived in a cottage at the top of a huge beanstalk. One sunny morning, they went for a walk in the woods to let their porridge cool down. A little girl was walking about and she smelt the porridge. She climbed up the beanstalk and she ate one of the bears' porridge. Then she went to sit down on one of the bears' chairs and she broke it. She went upstairs and got in one of the bears' beds. The girl was eaten by a wolf who was wearing a nightcap and dressing gown.

COREY JAMES HEWITT (15)
Barton Moss Education Unit, Manchester

HIDE, NOW!

As she creeps up the stairs you hide under your duvet because you know that the one that cackles is hunting you like you're a sitting duck, there's nowhere to run because the old hag is at your bedroom door. Hurry, play dead, do something - just don't move a muscle or you know what will happen. But it is too late. You just moved your right leg three inches left, there's no saving you from her wrath now.
'Jamie, you need to do your maths homework now.'
'I'll do it at 6 o'clock. Get out!'

JADE CASSIDY-ADAMS (15)
Baxter College, Kidderminster

RETURN TO MYSELF

Well, who came crawling back? Who is it now? No one I care about. A misty mind is better than an insane one. I run down the corridor, filthy floors beneath my feet. Cold goosebumps show up on my skin, like molehills. It is dark. Dim. I run past the mirror, a pen in my hand, an urge to stab. I want to feel pain, who is that crawling back? I look in a silver plate and see who. My sanity. Myself. Foggy head falling. I feel. See clear. Must return to the mist.

FAY GOERLACH (15)
Baxter College, Kidderminster

WOLFBLOOD

The wolf crept, composed, watching the human stalking silently through the bushes. The wolf was growling, the human turned around, holding the sword tightly. The wolf bared her teeth, snarling as it was a warning. Suddenly, she pounced, biting into the human's neck. The human was dead, blood pouring out of the human's neck. Looking down, the wolf was slashed in the leg, but she didn't care. The human's family never found the body. The wolf still creeps around. Now will you be the next victim of the wolfblood or will you be lucky enough to tell the tale?

OLIVIA ATHERTON (13)
Baxter College, Kidderminster

POWER OF GREED TO ANY PURE SOUL

A farmer lived a kind life, one night he was visited by the Devil. 'You never live until you live through rich eyes. Ten bottles to choose, nine honey, one poison. Drink honey, I'll give you gold.'
He drank one. 'It's honey!'
The Devil said, 'Call me to try again.'
Next day, he bought clothes, spent the rest on alcohol. When it ended, he called the Devil. Victory! Bought alcohol, did this till there were two bottles. 'What's this?'
The Devil replied, 'You don't recognise honey after so much alcohol. The alcohol's destroyed you! Be the monster greed made you.'

DANIEL CORREIA (15)
Baxter College, Kidderminster

HALF

It was a curse upon my mother. Birthed into water, shunned by light.
In a cave I now reside.
Waterlogged, water waist height, legs long since unravelled.
Pain, *swish*.
Often people come to look at me, oh yes, my 'pretty' face they'll see.
Pretty to them of course, but nay, not to me. Often, they'll ask me,
'Get out, come play.'
'No,' I'll say, 'I'll stay.'
Twisting, writhing, intestinal vines. Lift me out? Nay, lift them in. But
it's not as if they can swim.
In a cave I now reside. Flesh rising-scum on the surface. Friendless,
surrounded by corpses.

ELINOR NEVILLE (15)
Baxter College, Kidderminster

THE GIRL WITH THE VIOLET EYES

Plumes of smoke rose high into the sky, emanating from the burning bodies beneath. A young girl, hands dripping with blood, walks through the scorched remains of the townspeople. Not once does she falter at the blood on the sidewalk, or the lonely limbs strewn across the roads. Not once does she take her eyes off the looming dark figure at the centre of the destruction.
Reaching the figure, he lays a hand on her head, steadying her trembling body. She stops shaking. Her head twists sharply; I remember her vivid, violet eyes and then a bleak, cold nothingness.

KIRA MCLEAN (16)
Cardinal Newman Catholic School - A Specialist Science College, Luton

UNTITLED

He looked at Belle. Her eyes fluorescent oceans. 'Now the kiss that forever changes your life,' Belle whispered coarsely into the Beast's monstrous ears. However, Beast had different ideas. Belle didn't understand. He'd changed. Two-faced, his eyes had changed to the animal-red of a predator about to tear you to shreds. 'Answer me Beast!' she screamed with the ferocity of a lion.
As Beast turned to face her, he revealed the fangs which contained the sacred poison. 'No, you will be a beast forever!' he roared as he sank his fangs into Belle, forever turning her into a beast.

CAMERON PEARCEY (15)
Haybridge High School & Sixth Form, Stourbridge

THE LAST LITTLE PIG

The stench of blood chills me to the bone. My fortress is finalised - I'm taking every precaution I can. I set a trap for the wolf - the cauldron under the chimney should claim my vengeance. There is heavy breathing encircling the perimeter. Then, a hellish fury looks me in the eye through the window. My body viciously trembles at the sight of my predator. Relief follows as he scales the wall and powers his way toward the chimney: my plan is working. Violently, he fires down the chimney and lands in the water. It's cold; as am I, with horror.

CAVAN WEST (14)
Haybridge High School & Sixth Form, Stourbridge

CHOKED

'Rapunzel, Rapunzel, let down your golden hair!'
Deep, shaky breaths escaped a quivering body. Hair as yellow as
corn, a pale face of desperation. Words that echoed through her
mind at night; the burning desire for something she cannot help. Like
a person, forgotten, ignored.
The call entered the window once more; another eager plea.
A large lump formed in her throat, but she masked it quickly with a
gentle caress from a loop of hair - shining golden in the moonlight.
The prince stood below the window; awaiting the first sight of his true
love.
And then she jumped.

EMILY ANN MAE DENNIS (14)
Haybridge High School & Sixth Form, Stourbridge

THE ROSE

Under her spell, my pale finger brushed the sharpened tip of the
ruby-red rose. My eyes so transfixed on the dark blood that gently
dripped from my finger, I didn't notice the wall of roses that began
to flourish from the ground like a phoenix rising from a pool of ash.
Gazing down, my vision blurred, my hands went cold and my head
pounded. I felt as though my skull would burst. Something was
inside; something wanted to get out. My knees went weak and
I dropped to the floor, unaware that upon awakening I would be
trapped.

EVA GRAY (15)
Haybridge High School & Sixth Form, Stourbridge

Woodcutter

He had found them earlier, traipsing around the wild cattle let loose from their field. He hadn't fulfilled his promise - that was the worst part - he could simply have done it right then and there, but something stopped him. He turned on his heel and ran after them, as fast as the weighty lumber axe would allow him to do so. He thought of the money, of his new life, but something still bothered him. He came to a halt again and took the paper scrap out of his pocket. It read: 'Kill Hansel and Gretel'.

Felix Farrow (15)
Haybridge High School & Sixth Form, Stourbridge

Untitled

A putrid smell lingered in the room. I gagged. Shifting uncomfortably on the multiple mattresses beneath me, my curiosity overwhelmed me. What was underneath? I wasn't sure what to expect as I hesitantly pulled the mattresses from the towering pile. One by one, they slid off, the pile slowly diminishing. I gasped. The sickly stench burnt my nostrils and infected my lungs. Mangled, decaying corpses were carelessly strewn underneath my bed. My stomach twisted; all the corpses wore the same, luxurious dresses still clinging to their lifeless bodies, just like mine. The heavy door slammed. I knew I was next.

Grace Clifford (15)
Haybridge High School & Sixth Form, Stourbridge

HOOD

Cascading from the girl's delicate complexion, falls the hood from head to toe. Red of beauty, of love, of hate, walking through the grasping, glaring trees. The flowers, they sway through the evening breeze.

As the moon comes out to dance, so does the creature from within. But dance does not the girl, as at night the demons play. Eyes so rabid and claws sharp, the dripping teeth, snarling growls. Cascading from the wolf's menacing complexion, falls hopes and dreams, the long red cloak. Beware of the night: the dark. For it brings the beast inside Little Red Riding Hood.

JENNY KENDALL (15)
Haybridge High School & Sixth Form, Stourbridge

BEAUTY AND THE BEAST

As the piano began to play, the sun sank lower in the sky giving way to the velvety dark of night. Beast took Belle into his arms, sighing a happy sigh, and turned to Belle. She looked back and a steady stream of tears flowed its way down her pale cheeks. But through the tears, she smirked.

'Cheer up child, it'll turn out alright in the end. You'll see,' Mrs Potts said with an unusual grimace across her face.

Shortly after the blood had dried into the carpet, the piano started playing again.

Belle looked at Beast's lifeless body, emotionless.

KIA STARKS (14)
Haybridge High School & Sixth Form, Stourbridge

THE SHADOW

I looked up to see a dark looming shadow above me. I was intrigued as to what the shape was and why it was so foreign to me. Whirling through the waves I edged closer until I was as close as can be without getting caught. A murky shadow shifted and a hand plunged into the water. The wild hand pulled my fiery locks and twisted viciously like a lion attacking its prey. I twisted and writhed with terror, with no luck of getting away. Panic flooded through me. This was it. This was the end for me.

LUCY ROBSON (15)
Haybridge High School & Sixth Form, Stourbridge

OVERDOSE

As the clouds parted beneath her, Alice relaxed her muscles; she welcomed this feeling. Back in Wonderland again. As she surveyed the land below, a sense of relief came over her. They told her she wasn't allowed to come back here. She'd expected to have hit the ground by now... Alice could clearly see it beneath her but she wasn't getting any closer to it. Figures formed above her, 'Alice... can you hear me? Come back Alice,' their voices echoed. She knew she couldn't come back this time.
The doctor faced her father in the hospital, 'I'm sorry... she's gone.'

MADDIE BAKER (15)
Haybridge High School & Sixth Form, Stourbridge

A COLD WORD

'Please! I'm begging you!' yelled the Red Queen, as she lay, struggling and gasping for breath, 'It's her you want! She's pale and cold like ice; it's reflected in her malicious soul! Can't you see?' Her fiery eyes called out to Hatter - pleading for him to change his mind - but he was, quite literally, seeing red.
'Silence! I know what you've done.' Pausing for a moment, with a sudden swing of his sword, he yelled, 'Off with your head!' But he felt her bitter presence, her frozen breath on his neck. He was trapped in her world forever.

MAISIE RAWLE (15)
Haybridge High School & Sixth Form, Stourbridge

JACK HORNER

Little Jack Horner sat in a corner eating a Christmas pie. Manoeuvring left, left him short of breath and wheezing, he started to cry. As Little Jack Horner stayed in his corner, for that would never cease. His love of cake and pies, and such forsook him to be obese. Perhaps it was a miracle, perhaps it was a lie, but Jack Horner had a plan, for sugar never dies. Centuries Jack lived eating apples to the core. He ate for endless minutes till he couldn't anymore.

ROSE WINN (15)
Haybridge High School & Sixth Form, Stourbridge

Untitled

I have a cunning plan! As I saw her knelt down on the floor cradling her stomach, with devastation my plan hit me like a truck. A light bulb hovered over my head. I walked over to her, claiming to be her fairy godmother. All of a sudden, a glimmer of hope lit up her eyes, it was as if she believed I was going to help her. I waved my wand…
She was a horse! It worked! My masterplan had worked! The only reason she'd be heading to the ball was to drive the carriage for her stepsisters!

ELLA SOPHIE TOMLINSON (12)
Hope Academy, Newton-Le-Willows

Untitled

The prince whispered into Sleeping Beauty's ear, 'Go ahead, touch it.' Sleeping Beauty leant over and a small needle entered her finger. She collapsed, her eyes locked on the ceiling. They were slowly covered by a sheet of skin. 'I'll give you 20 gold pieces if you say you did it,' the prince said to a dark figure.
'Fine,' said a cackling voice.
The prince waited for a week and came to find Sleeping Beauty in a rose bed. He crept over and kissed her. As Sleeping Beauty awoke, the prince mumbled, 'Say a thing and I'll harm you.'

GRACE AMELIA BURNETT (12)
Hope Academy, Newton-Le-Willows

THE OPEN DOOR

I know I have to score big to prove them wrong, as I (Mike Wazowski) will attempt to surpass the all-time scaring record. Confidently, gladly, happily, I nervously crept to the door where it could all begin; my whole scaring career. Determination and perseverance are making me prove them wrong once and for all and make my family proud. However, mixed emotions tried to change the atmosphere as I finally crept into the unknown, unnatural human world. Agitated and petrified, every single bone in my body filled up with uncertainty. Nevertheless, I knew I had to soldier on.

THOMAS HARRY BENNETT (12)
Hope Academy, Newton-Le-Willows

I WAS READY

Ping! I was ready. They walked towards me. I could hear their voices and their footsteps, closer and closer they walked. Slowly, they opened the oven and pulled me out. I was ready. They watched me, mouths watering…

CHLOE NICOLE BRENDA FRAYNE (12)
Hope Academy, Newton-Le-Willows

UNTITLED

It appeared in front of the tall mushroom-shaped tower. 'Rapunzel, Rapunzel, let down your hair!' The prince watched as the beautiful strawberry strands flew out like a fluttering silk blanket. He took the silk between his hands and started to make his way up the tower. Step by step, he stomped his way up, eager to see his future bride. He reached the top and climbed over to see her sitting on a chair. But she wasn't what he had expected; her face was deformed... She was a man.

SAJIDAH RAHMAN (12)
Hope Academy, Newton-Le-Willows

UNTITLED

As I finally come out of the drop, I travel back to Gotham and get suited and kitted, ready to fight my rival, Bane. The city of good people and policemen went out to fight the thugs. I was fighting the thugs and came across Bane and instantly made eye contact, and started fighting. Then, as I knocked him down, he told me we were brothers...

SAM FAGAN
Hope Academy, Newton-Le-Willows

FINDING CORAL

'Dad! Dad! Wake up, it's time for school,' Nemo shouted to his dad. When Nemo arrived at school, he spotted something hiding in the anemone. Something that looked exactly like him, with the orange and white stripes. 'Who could it be? Why do they look like me?' As Nemo was talking to his teacher he saw them again. Nemo swam over with his little fin. Face-to-face they looked at each other. 'Could it really be you? Mum...?'

LUCY O'REILLY (14)
Hope Academy, Newton-Le-Willows

UNTITLED

Humpty Dumpty sat on a wall, Humpty Dumpty had a great fall. Did he do it himself or was he pushed? As the egg dripped out we stood up with joy. But why was he happy now? Now that's what no one knows!

DANIEL PHILIP RICHARDS (14)
Hope Academy, Newton-Le-Willows

Peter Pan Uncovered

Peter ran frantically, forcing the terrified, confused children to soar towards Neverland, or should it be called 'Never Come Back Land'? Children violently roared into the ground, tearing the turf away. Pitiless Peter threw cunning disguises on them and threw them aboard his rickety ship. Off it went, sailing into the forbidden abyss, where he would do horrible things to them. His manipulative fairy, hovering by his side, watched with a sharp eye. The hero swung in. The helpful Captain Hook was there to save the sneakily stolen children. But suddenly, a crocodile snapped him up. The children were doomed…

Tom Steven Burnett (12)
Hope Academy, Newton-Le-Willows

GUARDIAN ANGELS

Peter pointed to the house. 'The third window up, Tink,' whispered Peter pointing to a dimly-lit window. 'The window's open.' We flew silently towards the window. 'Wait here whilst I get them,' whispered Peter pointing to the side of the window. I waited. He came out of the window holding a young girl's hand. 'This is Wendy,' he said with a smile, then, 'this is Michael and this is John,' as two young boys clambered out of the window. 'Right, let's go to Neverland!' said Peter overexcited.

'But why?' said the young girl.

'Because you are no longer alive.'

ELLIE SHARD (12)
Hope Academy, Newton-Le-Willows

The Undercover Big Bad Wolf

The big bad wolf turned out to be an undercover wolf. He couldn't be bad because he was a person that dressed up and everyone believed that he was real. He turned out to have asthma so couldn't blow up Grandma's house otherwise he would be killing himself in an unusual way. In the end it turned out that the wolf was Little Red Riding Hood trying to kill her grandma because she hated her. Little Red Riding Hood eventually got her way by putting her harming claws around her neck, forcing the blood out for her to be dead.

Leah Blinstone (12)
Hope Academy, Newton-Le-Willows

Sleeping Beauty With A Twist

She woke up, thought life was great and stood up with a spring in her step. Then she stopped. Sleeping Beauty's whole world just fell apart, the evil Maleficent was after her… How could she forget? As she opened the door, she saw the evil glare of Maleficent. She slammed the door shut. When would Maleficent finally get her?

Keira Louise Blood (12)
Hope Academy, Newton-Le-Willows

THE THEORY BEHIND WOODY, LOTSO BEAR AND BEAU!

I knew something was wrong. I discovered feelings in my head. A boy smelling of strawberries, he was up to something. He started to turn pink; the colour rising through his body. I turned suddenly and he escaped quickly. My sister, Beau, had been missing for weeks and we had placed 'missing person' posters around all areas. Where could she be?

Oh no, this can't be right! I am trapped in a box! I can feel shiny, hard skin. I look up and realise that maybe I'm not human anymore!

ALEX HAYDEN (12)
Hope Academy, Newton-Le-Willows

CRAZY PEOPLE

In the ancient castle, there's a young girl who spends most of her time sitting around talking to the furniture. She sings to the cups, gossips to the candelabra and dances with the clocks. She has never left the castle since the day she entered. The people in the town call her crazy, insane and ill as she is in love with a dog and claims he's a prince.

However, there was never a castle in this town... so who's the crazy one now?

MEGAN LOUISE THORPE (13)
Hope Academy, Newton-Le-Willows

ROBIN HIS DREAMS

One dark night in Gotham, Robin was running along the rooftops. Suddenly Wolverine jumped out of nowhere and tried to kill Robin, but Robin moved out the way and got to the batcave. There, instead of Batman, it was Sherlock. Robin said, 'What's going on?' Sherlock replied, 'Say, what are you wearing Watson and why do you look younger?'
Robin was still panicking. Wolverine opened the door but then he turned into a wolf. They drove away, that's when Superman came and ripped the wolf in half. Robin was relieved when a knight came and stabbed him.

LESLIE CALVIN KARA (13)
Hope Academy, Newton-Le-Willows

CINDERELLA

The clock struck 12, Cinderella came out. She saw the bomb in the black, dull clock. She ran as quickly as she could. Her old, rotten shoe came off and she did not realise that her shoe had come off. But when she got in her sparkling carriage the bomb finally blew up.

SHANNON SMITH (13)
Hope Academy, Newton-Le-Willows

THE PIGS' PROBLEMS

My family got kicked out of their home so they decided to build a house but my two brothers had an argument about what to build their house out of, so they built one each. One of my brothers built their house out of straw but couldn't afford the rent so he destroyed it and blamed the wolf. My other brother made a house out of sticks and he went out, came back and the wind had blown the house down, but he thought it was the wolf. They took the wolf to court, he wasn't guilty, he owed nothing.

AOLANI LOUISE KINSEY (13)
Hope Academy, Newton-Le-Willows

TRICKS OVER THE MIND

What is that you think you see? You look once and then it's gone.
'Why have you stopped?' asked Jasmine. Aladdin looked as pale as a ghost. 'The Genie is here, but it's not possible, he died!'
Jasmine looked around and saw nothing - 'It must be your mind dear.'
'He's here waving, his face so morbid,' he said scared that he was being haunted.
The truth was the Genie never died, he just played tricks on Aladdin so he would never forget about him.

BRANDON STOKES (12)
Hope Academy, Newton-Le-Willows

LIES FROM GAMBLING

My life was perfect until I found out about a secret, a secret which changed my life forever. I was only small when I was stolen, however I wasn't stolen. They knew, my so-perfect family knew, that witch was going to take me. The truth hurts badly, my father and mother giving me over to such a beast. The witch won, she won me, by gambling. While my parents were left with no money and no little girl.

REBECCA HEATON (13)
Hope Academy, Newton-Le-Willows

GUARDS OF THE TOWER

The princess was locked high at the top of the tallest tower. In a deep, deep sleep. Waiting to be awoken by true love's kiss. Prince after prince after prince attempted to reach the princess. However, the tower was also under Maleficent's curse and guarded by two huge ogres. Never to be released. Small countries would disappear from attempts to rescue the beautiful princess. It got past her 20th birthday and many centuries passed. The princess was slowly fading away, hunger and dehydration crept upon the princess. Will she ever get rescued? Will we ever know if she does?

PHOEBE CHANDLER (13)
Hope Academy, Newton-Le-Willows

UNTITLED

Batman was in his secret base when he got an emergency. So he put on his suit and flew out the window to go find someone who was in trouble. When he got there The Joker was there with a girl who was in trouble. So he ran up to The Joker and kicked him into a pool of lava then he flew to the girl and took her home. And when they got there Batman got loads of money for saving her.

MATTHEW EDWARDS (13)
Hope Academy, Newton-Le-Willows

UNTITLED

As the toy group jumped over the burning flame and dodged The Crusher, suddenly they dropped. The whole group found themselves gazing into a hole and before they knew it, they were dead. The group were melted down and made into a bomb, saved for a special occasion. At last, the bomb exploded in the USA.

LIAM LUPTON
Hope Academy, Newton-Le-Willows

Olaf's Life

Olaf woke up and thought, *I want to go to the beach.* So he got up and packed his suitcase. While he was on his way he met Donkey. Donkey was really hot so Olaf got his bag and gave Donkey his water. 'Is that better?' They got to the beach and relaxed.

CHLOE WHITELEY (13)
Hope Academy, Newton-Le-Willows

Cinder Hell No!

She waltzed in, looking for the man of her dreams. There he was, the prince, with his back towards her.
'Erm... hello?' she muttered.
He turned around and nearly knocked her out with is breath. 'Sup?'
They started dancing but the mole on the end of his nose kept poking her in the eye. The bell struck twelve so she ran for it, leaving a shoe behind.
The prince was at the door!
Why oh why did she let him try the shoe on her?

JOE ABERNETHY (12)
Hope Academy, Newton-Le-Willows

UNTITLED

There he was, the big green animal stood there with glasses of milk. We guarded the king of all gingerbreads from the milk as this would melt him. At the side of the green blob stood a very crazy donkey singing the most annoying song. Our front four men started charging at the beast, aggressively. He started to throw a couple of glasses of milk... A drop of milk hit the king and tragedy struck, the king started to melt.

NATHAN BEVAN (12)
Hope Academy, Newton-Le-Willows

DEAD RED RIDING HOOD

I heard the screams come from the house, I walked over to the house with my axe. I thought to myself, *what's going on here?* I smashed down the door and saw a wolf and a girl.
The wolf said, 'I'm sorry, I'm hungry.'
'It's fine,' I said. Then I realised that it was a wolf that talked, I had always wanted a talking wolf. I cut off the girl's head and took the wolf as a pet. I lived happily after.

JOSEPH THOMAS ROBERT CHARLESTON (12)
Hope Academy, Newton-Le-Willows

Our Wonderful King...

My name is Pagan Min, creator of the rebellion named 'The Golden Path'. The rebellion was to take down the king, Ajay Ghale, that is my goal. He came into play after he greedily took the throne after he murdered his father, Mohan Ghale. He was kind to others lower than himself, such as us civilians. He came one day and killed my family in front of me; then said to me, 'Now boy, you will join me or you will end up like them.' I then vowed to kill him and created my rebellion to avenge my family...

BRADLEY HARRISON (12)
Hope Academy, Newton-Le-Willows

Down The Rabbit Hole

Trepidation filled me as I didn't know what to expect next. That little rabbit, in his white waistcoat kept muttering, 'We're going to be late, late!'
Frantically I hurried after him, not wanting to upset my new friend. Suddenly he stopped; I followed suit shortly after and was left awestruck at the gaping hole that was beneath my feet. 'Do we jump?' I asked.
'You do,' and I was left tumbling into the darkness below.
Light streamed onto my face. I glanced around and what I saw amazed me. My family. My friends. A hospital room.

CHLOE HOOPER (12)
Hope Academy, Newton-Le-Willows

GOOD OR EVIL?

Once upon a time, there lived two girls. One good and one evil. Every year, a schoolmaster comes to a village and selects one of the most evil and good children. One of the girls had always longed to go to the school of good but the other girl wanted to stay in the village. One night, there was a loud silence. The schoolmaster was there. He swooped the two girls off their feet and rushed them off to the school of good and evil. They fell into the schools. Cinderella, good? But she was bad. Stepmother evil? She's good!

GABRIELLE ROSE BARNES (12)
Hope Academy, Newton-Le-Willows

UNTITLED

Little Red Riding Hood was walking through the woods to go to her grandma's and give her some cookies, when suddenly the wolf got a scent of the cookies. He sprinted through the woods and spotted Little Red Riding Hood. The wolf quickly ran up behind Little Red Riding Hood and swallowed her in one! Then he got dressed into her clothes and kept walking round to find Grandma's house until finally he found it and like he did to Little Red Riding Hood, he swallowed Grandma in one, then sat on the bed and ate all of the cookies.

DANIEL HILL (13)
Hope Academy, Newton-Le-Willows

THE DEVIL'S DAUGHTER

The wolf caught a scent. Following the scent led him deeper into the forest. He didn't seem to mind because he was born in the forest. He knew his way round. Not long afterwards, he saw a young girl surrounding him. He ran, running after his prey. His prey was a small girl, as he got closer he realised that she wasn't running so, nervously, the wolf slowly approached and she turned slowly, showing her face. He gasped, her face was lifeless. Her eyes were all black, he knew it was the end.

ROSS ANTHONY BOOTH (13)
Hope Academy, Newton-Le-Willows

BIG BAD WOLF

It was just a normal day, well that was what she thought. When her mum gave her the cookies she ran off into the woods, but what she didn't know was that was the last time she would see her mum because the wolf gobbled her in one go. Then the bloodthirsty wolf sprinted to Grandma's house and gobbled her up in one. But the wolf wanted one more person to eat, so he waited for the girl and then the rest is history.

ALEX SKEECH (13)
Hope Academy, Newton-Le-Willows

54

GRIMM BROTHERS - RAPUNZEL

There it was, before my very eyes, the most known tower in the entire kingdom. It was rumoured to be home to the fairest maiden in the land. Hair as yellow as corn was meant to be dangling down for me to climb but there was none. Luckily, there were stairs on the other side of the building, so I went up them.

I opened the previously locked door, to find a beautiful girl hanging from the ceiling. Her face was as white as snow and she showed no sign of life. She had used her hair as a rope.

POPPY PARK
John Masefield High School, Ledbury

FAIRY TALE

Through the forest, past the river, over the wall - the prince runs to the tower he'd climbed yesterday to see a beautiful princess. Like the previous day, he shouts, 'Rapunzel, Rapunzel, let down your hair!'

A long waterfall of golden hair cascades down the side of the tower, which the prince determinedly climbs, eager to reach the prize.

When he's near the top, he sees a face emerge, but not what he's expecting: an ugly warty face. The witch at the top cackles evilly, as she throws off her golden wig, sending the prince tumbling down to his painful death.

AMY HILL
John Masefield High School, Ledbury

THE GINGERBREAD MAN AND THE AK-47

The trap was set. 'You can't catch me, I'm the gingerbread man!' the gingerbread man called cheerfully as he lightly jogged down the grassy lane. As the gingerbread man turned the corner an evil smile came across his face.
The baker dashed around the corner after him. Quickly, the gingerbread man slid under the trap wire, it was too late for the baker. As his foot caught the trap wire he was greeted with fifty shots to the head by the AK-47 attached to the trap wire. The gingerbread man chuckled. 'He will cook nicely... '

JOSEPH BARTHOLOMEW
Kenilworth School & Sports College, Kenilworth

DEADLY DUMPTY

Humpty Dumpty sat on the wall, Humpty Dumpty had a big fall. Humpty didn't break though. While he was brushing all of the dust off himself he noticed a crack on his side. Then he wondered, *shouldn't I be dripping yolk?* Then Humpty fell to the floor screaming. Humpty was no more. A baby goose had hatched from inside Humpty. It was yellow-grey with a yellow beak. It headed to the market. It jumped on the butcher and shredded him to pieces. It was never seen again but it is said it will return again.

JEEVAN SINGH VIRDI (13)
Kenilworth School & Sports College, Kenilworth

You Thought You Knew Me!

I entered my room, happy to see Woody and Jessie smiling at me from the shelf opposite the window in our big, new house. 'Come and get your dinner Andy.' I scrambled downstairs for my spaghetti Bolognese. After, I dragged myself up the stairs once again. I stepped onto the blue carpet of my bedroom and shut my door, staring out that same window. Then I saw it... Woody and Jessie outside the window, but this time they were bold-eyed, holding a knife. I was about to scream when I noticed it wasn't a window, it was a mirror...

Tia Rose Eales (15)
Kenilworth School & Sports College, Kenilworth

The Sea's Death Angel

Wave after wave, he saw no sight of her. He was remembering her sweet harmonic voice as she sang. There was a girl covered in a white sheet tied with ropes, her red hair flowing, he thought to himself that she was the one. He started running towards her but then she darted over and he saw a horrid face, her eyes were black and bruised, she had cuts all over, she was staring at him. A deathly hollow look. She muttered, 'I seek revenge because of you!' She pulled him against the sea as the wave rose! Gone, dead!

Zaynab Iqbal (12)
Kenilworth School & Sports College, Kenilworth

A Tale Of Loss

There he was. Arjan. I watched as he entered the abandoned house. He acted possessed, chanting 'chicken' upon his every move. It all made sense though, as the house was previously owned by a chicken farmer. Don't ask how I know that. Silence. The clocks stopped ticking. Arjan slowly decided to back out of the house. That was until... *thud!* The front door shut. As the house darkened, all the internal doors opened. Arjan was foolish enough to go upstairs and go into the only room that was closed: the closet. And from that moment onwards, Arjan was no more.

ONKAR MATHARU (14)
Kenilworth School & Sports College, Kenilworth

What Happened, Aurora?

She had been such a sweet little girl. Beautiful blonde hair with blue eyes and pale skin. Her cheeks used to be rosy red. Nowadays, they're tearstained, with thick, black, bold lines on her eyelids. She loves her piercings. She's got seven; three are self-pierced. It was one of these that shut her eyes forever. The prick of the safety pin put her into a never-ending sleep. They say that a true love can end the sleep; but what does one do in a society where there is no such thing as true love?

AMY GOODWIN (14)
Kenilworth School & Sports College, Kenilworth

GOODBYE SISTER

He had reached the clearing. He jumped, catching her hair in his hands. He climbed. A howl erupted from the undergrowth into the night. He turned, half slipping but kept climbing. Pattering feet, something burst through the thorns. A wolf. There was a haunted look in its eyes. The wolf sprang at the hair, the girl screamed as it ripped. The boy fell and snapped. The wolf fell, shot dead. A young girl stepped out of the thorns, pulled back her red hooded cloak and smiled. She knocked another arrow. 'Goodbye Sister.'

HANNAH MATTHEWS (14)
Kenilworth School & Sports College, Kenilworth

RAPUNZEL'S PRINCE

There was once a young girl who had been locked in a tower by an evil witch. The witch kept her locked away from the world and treated her harshly like a slave. Her name was Rapunzel and she had long golden hair.
One day, a prince saw Rapunzel in the tower and climbed up towards her. Then he drew his knife and cut her hair. Hearing her screams, the witch ran up the stairs and pushed the prince out of the tower window. The witch had saved Rapunzel from the horrible prince and they lived happily ever after.

AMY HALL (14)
Kenilworth School & Sports College, Kenilworth

THE THIEF

Crunch! The man's shovel had hit rock bottom. He heaved open the box and then saw the thing that would change his life... Screaming in delight, the man grabbed a handful of the gold, threw it up in the air but he was surprised when the tingle of money hitting the floor sounded like a gunshot. He knew death was upon him when he looked down, just beneath his diaphragm; a stream of blood came pouring out, all over his glistening white shirt. A depressing thud came upon the quiet air as he fell to the ground. 'Never ever steal... '

HENRY MAGGS (14)
Kenilworth School & Sports College, Kenilworth

CINDERELLA'S BAD PARTY

Cinderella's stepmother and sisters wouldn't let her go to the party. She cried by the fireplace and suddenly a fairy appeared and said, 'You shall go to the party,' and then her bike became a limo and her gown became a dress.
She rode to the party and she saw the front door and there were no signs. She knocked on the door and it opened. She looked around and in the living room there was everyone. They were reading, this wasn't a party, it was a book club, so she went home sad and disappointed... No prince!

ENRICO BUCCI (14)
Kenilworth School & Sports College, Kenilworth

RAPUNZEL'S NIGHTMARE

She stands with her long golden locks of hair in her hand, she contemplates whether her decision is right. Letting it go, the hair that used to drop down her back to the floor, just falls to the ground along with the scissors.

Her dream is not right that night. 'Rapunzel, Rapunzel, let down your hair.' The same dream every night. She stares over the balcony, twists her head to let down her hair. But it's changed; her hair barely passes her shoulders. It's gone. The dream wasn't a dream, it was reality. Her dream was real, the worst nightmare.

JODIE WARD (14)
Kenilworth School & Sports College, Kenilworth

PRINCE CHARMING

Waiting hopelessly in the tower I was bracing myself for the appearance of my prince charming. Hours passed, I saw a glimpse of a shadow from the corner of my eye, a heavy breath was released down upon my shoulder. I was being watched. Violently, I spun round in shock to see who had been stalking me. 'My prince!' Delighted, I sprang forward. Yet I was not to know what hit me next. I gazed down towards my feet, blood was oozing out of my wounded stomach. Starting to collapse with my last breath I peered up and stuttered, 'Why?'

LULABELLE THOMAS-MANUEL (14)
Kenilworth School & Sports College, Kenilworth

THE BEAUTIFUL BEAST AND THE BEASTLY BEAUTY

As the last rose petal plucked itself from its stem and slowly settled on the table below, a tear ran down the beast's face; he knew that his time had run out! Suddenly, he saw his only hope return to the castle but she was not back to save him. When she reached the forbidden West Wing, she saw the beast standing over the rose, he didn't say anything to her, he just wept. This increased her anger so she took a firm hold of her dagger and let go; the last thing he saw was the beauty's beastly reflection!

CHARLIE MAY NICHOLLS (13)
Kenilworth School & Sports College, Kenilworth

LITTLE BEGGAR

The beautiful mermaid crawled out of the ocean. Her chest tightened, her breathing became heavy panting, she realised this could be it, her one true love... She waited and waited in the glaring sun. Her soft fingertips brushed past her dried lips, her tail looked like a giant pile of stones. The mermaid closed her eyes and took one last sad breath. The prince encountered the sizzling body, slashed her tail and yanked her beach-waved hair. He rode off, leaving the lifeless body behind. The prince turned into a murderer and the innocent turned into a victim.

HOLLY COOP (12)
Kenilworth School & Sports College, Kenilworth

THE COLD DARK CASTLE

The gates opened, ready for the human eyes to see. Everyone's poor souls walked in with faces of excitement, greeting everyone with ice hands covered with silk gloves. Looking over her shoulder she gave her sister the signal. Elsa was slowly taking her silk gloves off and the castle gates closed. The room went dark and a gun had been shot. Screams came out and everyone was frozen. The sisters took the children, knots tied and no escape, they took their bite. *Crunch!* The blood oozed out like a river. They whispered, 'Night, night, sleep tonight, take care every night.'

ZOE WILKINSON (13)
Kenilworth School & Sports College, Kenilworth

POOR MISS WHITE

She was a ghost, sprinting through the trees. Her life at stake. She could hear the stomping of the hunter behind her. What was that tall building with a small door? She didn't care, she would do anything to escape the hunter. She scrambled inside, something wasn't quite right. She was not alone. There was a creak of a floorboard behind her. She turned to see seven little dwarfs. They smiled. They gave her a bed, fed her up and waited for her to sleep. Then sliced out her heart. The hunter was trying to help. Poor Miss White.

ISABELLE DORRINGTON (13)
Kenilworth School & Sports College, Kenilworth

Forgotten Beauty

Silently waiting, stiff and crooked, hidden beneath a beautiful but deceitful figure. The girl was left in the shadows, forgotten. An orange tinge flooded the horizon, the new day approached, but her faith had died. Her hope slowly slipped away, but little did she know there was someone... the tall figure of a man challenged his way to the tower, to find the motionless girl, the man was not the prince to save her life... but instead to end it. He viciously gorged on her flesh, blood pouring from her wounds, leaving her dead and alone in her eternal slumber!

CHARLIE SIMCOX (13)
Kenilworth School & Sports College, Kenilworth

Super Humpty Dumpty

Humpty Dumpty sat on the wall. At night he had a fall. Luckily to Humpty's delight, the SWAT team rescued him. They took him back to their secret base, where he demanded some protection. After some persuasion they assembled a suit of armour. Humpty agreed and put on his suit. His first night was fine, the second was different. He fell off with such speed the armour broke. When the SWAT team found him, they were very annoyed with him. So they got out a bazooka and blew him up. They enjoyed eating him as well after that.

AARON WHITEHOUSE POPE (14)
Kenilworth School & Sports College, Kenilworth

PUSS IN BLOOD-GUTS IN BOOTS

The sweet little kitty sang a ditty in his baby boots. Carrying his sword he came across a manor belonging to the ruler of his country. He strolled inside. Peering through a door he noticed twenty maids and the emperor's butler. Swinging his sword whilst they slept, he vanquished them all, their blood, along with guts, drizzled out from them. The cat saw the king in his chambers, he ran up to the man, slaying his head from the rest of him, blood from his neck spontaneously exploded, our hero sprang onto the king's lap, sleeping with a soundless purr.

LUCY WOODWARD (13)
Kenilworth School & Sports College, Kenilworth

HIM AND THE BEAST

Once upon a time, in a little town in France, lived Maurice and Belle, Belle was beautiful and Gaston loved her. He wanted to marry her. Belle went into the forest, Gaston was following her. She saw a castle and was welcomed by dancing tea cups. The Beast glanced down at them, ran past Belle and fell instantly in love with Gaston.

JESSICA PECK (14)
Kenilworth School & Sports College, Kenilworth

Pinocchio Teaches Donkey A Lesson

Pinocchio was angry. Everyone was laughing at him, nobody was on his side, well no more. He had come up with an elaborate plan to get revenge, it was a faultless, perfect plan which could not fail. 'Why do you look like a girl, long nose?' shouted Donkey, beckoning the crowd.

'I don't!' exploded Pinocchio, whilst grasping his elongated nose, snapping it off and beginning to stab all the members of the crowd. He left Donkey for last, he grabbed Donkey by his grey ears, forcing his wooden nose down Donkey's throat, puncturing his lungs and brutally slaughtering his friend!

Joshua Daniel Hardy Butler (14)
Kenilworth School & Sports College, Kenilworth

SNOW WHITE AND THE FINAL FEAST

Running quickly through gloomy dark woods, Snow White searched for somewhere safe to stay, not to be hunted down by her stepmother's guards. Scared out of her wits, Snow White, after two days of searching, couldn't find anywhere to stay. Eventually, Snow White came across a small cottage on the outskirts of the wood. She found seven little men who let her stay and invited her for dinner.

'What are we having?' she asked excitedly.

The little men grinned, 'You!'

In the distance, Snow White's stepmother heard the painful scream and smiled with joy.

KATIE MAY STOCKBRIDGE (14)
Kenilworth School & Sports College, Kenilworth

THE TREES HAVE EYES

The little girl skipped in the shaded meadow, happy. She gathered fresh summer fruits and flowers, as a gift for her grandmother. But then, as she turned, she was shocked. The trees had moved. They were guarding the path she had taken. The sky darkened. She panicked and turned around. She heard a sinister snarl. She turned again and, to her horror, the trees were now blocking the path. They had moved again. She saw a shadow, with sinister yellow eyes. It moved closer, closer and closer still, running. It leapt. It was the last thing the girl ever saw.

LOUIS PERRY (14)
Kenilworth School & Sports College, Kenilworth

IF THE BOOT FITS

Cinderella was ecstatic, the prince was touring the country, looking for the girl who left her shoe. This would change her life for ever. She would be free, away from this house. A knock at the door, he was here, she ran downstairs. But as she attempted to pat the crystal slipper on, it didn't fit! It was then she realised her foot was swollen from running home with only one shoe on. She cried out. 'It was me!' Nobody would believe her.
'It can't be...' the prince said, placing the shoe perfectly on her stepsister's foot.

MEGAN HEATH (14)
Kenilworth School & Sports College, Kenilworth

LITTLE DEAD CREEPY KID

The demonic little girl hopped along the path slowly through the forest. She looked around curiously. She was meant to go to her grandma's house but never did. She stood under her favourite tree and talked to herself as if there was someone there. Her red coat was swishing around everywhere. A wolf! It jumped out on her; tearing her apart, she just laughed and laughed. How wonderful, a wolf was eating her. The blood oozed out of her body. She carried on laughing until she died. She got named 'Little Dead Creepy Kid'.

ALEXANDRA SCOTT (14)
Kenilworth School & Sports College, Kenilworth

HUMPTY DUMPTY, NEVER SEEN AGAIN

Humpty Dumpty was on a walk. He stumbled across a wall, it looked a bit tattered, however it was the right height for Humpty Dumpty. Humpty sat on the wall to have his lunch. He got his lunch box out to hear a sudden crack. The wall fell down with a mighty crash and Humpty fell down with it. Humpty was dead. Some soldiers found him, not knowing that it was Humpty so they retrieved the giant egg. They took him back and turned him into scrambled egg to have for dinner. Humpty Dumpty was never to be seen again.

ALEXANDER DARLOW (14)
Kenilworth School & Sports College, Kenilworth

69

SISTER NO MORE

She was my sister, there until the end. But she had been turned. Owls hooted, the wind howled. Then we saw the place that changed our lives. A single bite from the witch was all it took. Cupcakes, my only defence. I shoved my sister into the cage where I had been kept for days. I pushed the cake stand against the door. I stabbed the neck of the witch with a piece of glass and pushed her into the oven I should've died in. Screams shattered sugar-coated windows, I am no longer a little boy.

ISABELLE PERRY (13)
Kenilworth School & Sports College, Kenilworth

UNTITLED

She lies white as snow, waiting for her prince to come. Her Prince Charming arrives, leans over to kiss her but he turns to see behind him, a short man. They instantly fall in love, leaving Snow White to die, the not-so Prince Charming rides off into the sunset with Happy, the dwarf.

ERIN MYLES (13)
Kenilworth School & Sports College, Kenilworth

TERROR OF WOLF

The wolf's teeth shining, his eyes glazing, the three little pigs terrified. The wolf pushed them in the house and it went silent. The wolf emerged, covered in blood. A beautiful girl came along and the wolf jumped out at her, she screamed and he said, 'I love your dress and your lovely blowing hair.' The wolf said, 'Would you like to come in for tea?'

Cinderella said, 'I'd be delighted to.'

It started to thunder. He dragged her inside, there was a massive bang and Cinderella was never seen again.

KEELEY DAVIS (13)
Kenilworth School & Sports College, Kenilworth

THE DREAM COMING TO LIFE!

Her hair blew everywhere. Tired and exhausted she drifted down the staircase and fell into her lover's arms. But oh no! The glass slipper fell from her foot and smashed. Her dreams shattered with it. In her thoughts she'd begun to imagine getting out of this prison but now her chances were slim. She'd always wanted to be treated fairly not like the slave she'd become. Cinderella had tried to retrieve the other glass slipper but to no avail. It had dissolved into thin air, right before her very eyes. She realised now her life was never going to change!

KATIE COULTER (13)
Kenilworth School & Sports College, Kenilworth

Snow And Sleepy

She lay there. As still as the night, on a bed of brightly coloured flowers. Her hair black as a raven, lips red as blood, skin white as snow. The sun shone down on her, lighting up her face. The prince ran to her, a single teardrop trickled down his pale face. 'Snow,' he said. He gently kissed her on the lips. Her eyes slowly flickered open. She sat up ever so carefully. The prince took Snow in his arms. She refused. 'I'm sorry,' she said, 'but my heart belongs to Sleepy.'

ELISE HERRINGTON
Kenilworth School & Sports College, Kenilworth

The Seven Evil Dwarfs

She stood frail, she looked up to the huntsman, his hands around her neck. She could feel him panting on her face. As he lifted his knife, his eyes softened. He said, 'I can't, you're too beautiful, run, the queen's after you.'
She ran, perplexed at what the huntsman had revealed. As she caught her breath, seven dwarfs came from behind the bushes. Petrified, she stood there. Axes in hand, pointy hats, razor-red eyes, ready to kill...

IONA WARD (12)
Kenilworth School & Sports College, Kenilworth

UNTITLED

He dropped the bean into an open space in the ground and poured a small amount of water into the hole. He awoke the next morning with a shadow over his body, he curiously crept outside and saw the massive beanstalk. Then he grabbed a bag and started climbing. He grabbed the small branches, struggling his way up. He got halfway so he rested on a branch when suddenly he saw a massive green object falling from the sky. It landed on his house with his whole family inside. Suddenly, the beanstalk fell and Jack fell with it, to death.

JORDAN HOWES
Kenilworth School & Sports College, Kenilworth

HICKORY DICKORY DOCK

Hickory dickory dock. The man raced up the clock. And against it... Terrified at what he might see, he dared not turn around. He was being chased by something and it was only a matter of time. He was running up the centre of the clock tower, petrified by the thought of jagged teeth tearing into his flesh. Repeatedly stepping and stumbling but not getting any further away from the creature; he got to the top of the tower. But where was the creature?
He awoke... The creature was waiting in front of him; brandishing his bloodthirsty claws...

JOSEPH GREEN (12)
Manchester Health Academy, Manchester

THE CASTLE

So my best friend's mum is engaged to a prince. She invited me to stay the night in their castle. I didn't know she meant *forever!* The castle was overwhelming but also welcoming. I wandered around the empty corridors with my footsteps echoing through the castle. I heard whimpering from inside the walls. I desperately tried to get in but her mum's boyfriend was there. He smiled revealing fangs. I screamed as he bit me. I woke up inside the walls. I was the one I heard scream before. I was trapped.

TAYLOR HICKFORD
Manchester Health Academy, Manchester

SPLIT ENDS

I had killed Mother Gothel. Gone from my life, finally! Looking behind me I could see her blood-soaked clothes. She was dead alright. Taking a seat, a sigh of relief escaped my mouth. Looking around the room, I saw blood splattered everywhere. Next thing I knew, my long glossy hair was wrapped around my neck. Craning my head round, I saw Mother Gothel! As I strained, the latched hair scraped the skin from my neck. Small tears rolled down my cheeks, until everything was black and I had forgotten all. How could she? She was dead! We'll never know...

HANNAH BINDON (14)
Manchester Health Academy, Manchester

THE THREE BEARS

When Goldilocks went to the house of the bears, what did her blue eyes see? A family of contemptuous, fear-inducing grizzly bears. Foam dripping from their mouths. Snarls ringing around the room, the beasts took one look at Goldilocks and charged. Lunging behind a large chair, Goldilocks screamed in fear. You could see the whites of the demon's eyes. Smell the odour of death. Somehow, the primrose-haired girl made her way into the kitchen. Maggots and old fish heads littered the three large bowls on the table. Panicking, Goldilocks picked up a knife and prepared for a fight...

EMILY MATTHEWS (14)
Manchester Health Academy, Manchester

UNTITLED

As the summer ball drew closer, the desperation engulfed the girls. No way was Cinderella finding love before them! Surely there was a way to destroy her future. Thoughts gathered into their twisted minds. Eventually they came up with a perfect plan. Cinderella owned an astonishing pair of glass slippers. All they had to do was find a way to fit the shoe on their huge feet. Anastasia came up with an idea. 'Let's cut our feet down!' They grabbed the sharpest knife possible and began slicing down their toes...

LAUREN FIELDING (14)
Manchester Health Academy, Manchester

THAT WAS IT

Hysterically, Micky strolled down the abandoned street as he thought of all the tragic events that happened; he loved Minnie but he lost her… Suicidal thoughts went through his head as he couldn't think why she cheated. Slowly, he carried on walking down that never-ending road, tears trickling down his face. He knew he was going to kill himself. He had nothing left. He was lost without her. Micky couldn't bear seeing her happily settled with someone else. Slowly, he approached the bridge; it was time to go. Micky slowly walked towards the edge. That was it. He jumped.

HANNAH BENTHAM (14)
Manchester Health Academy, Manchester

TOO LATE

Falling. I was falling to my doom. I jolted awake. It was just a nightmare. I got dressed and went to the woods to interpret my dream. I was unaware of the danger that lurked there. All I knew was that every time I went there I was being watched. I turned around and saw two red eyes glaring back at me. I did not shake in fear. I stood my ground. The eyes kept on moving towards me. The large demon wolf strolled towards me. The falling dream was a warning to me. I was too late to react...

KATE WILSON (14)
Manchester Health Academy, Manchester

SORROWFUL SNOW WHITE

I am the 8th dwarf, seeing a woman on my bed. I lurk closer but Doc plunges me into darkness as she awakens; white skin, black hair. The dwarfs leave; Angry grabs me threatening, 'Touch Snow and you're dead!' Sneakily, we speak, becoming instant friends. Slowly, falling in love…
One day, a mysterious hag opens the door, offering poisoned apples. Tricked, Snow collapses and I painfully remember Doc sneering, 'Find a lover and leave!' I have found her… Prince kisses her. No effect.
With one last breath I say, 'I shall follow my love.' Slowly I bite into the apple…

NICOL RAD (12)
Manchester Health Academy, Manchester

CLIFFORD JUMPER GOES SPLAT

Clifford Jumper loved danger. He began by jumping over cows' backs; then from houses in the village. Every day people would tell him that he'd gone too far this time. And every day he'd land with a bump and a bruise but stagger home to his children for supper. Over time his tricks became old, so he set off over the hills in search of a new quest. When he did not return, they looked for him. And after all they did find him, but they told his family otherwise; as this was the better of two tragedies.

HARRY WOOLDRIDGE
Meadowhead School, Sheffield

THE EMPIRE

Caesar wished for freedom, to free his people, suppressed by fear of 'The Empire' who had enslaved them. They offered him a daring proposition; he must return a much-respected relic which would remove the slave laws opposed upon them. He accepted, wanting to impress his dear Martha.
Riding through marshes and woods upon his trusty steed, he despaired greatly. There was no relic to be found. He returned, disappointed and broken, only to discover the mass slaughter of his people, Martha included, by 'The Empire'. A fierce battle ensued; Caesar had nothing but vengeance on his mind...

JOSH AISTHORPE (17)
Rainsbrook Secure Training Centre, Rugby

THE THREE BIG PIGS

One day, three big pigs were looking for wolves to kill, when suddenly they saw a puff of smoke where someone had seen the pigs and ran. They could not see the person but they chased the smoke frantically. They saw a wolf huffing and puffing trying to hide in a house of straw, but it was huffing and puffing that much that it huffed and puffed the house down. It tried to run again, but before it could run into a house of bricks, the gangster pigs were called, and killed the wolf before it could cause anymore antics.

ALEX SMITH (16)
Rainsbrook Secure Training Centre, Rugby

TWISTED FAIRY TALE

Once upon a time, there was a gingerbread man who turned into a wolf at night. Everybody needed to lock their doors and windows so they didn't get eaten. He looked sweet on the outside but on the inside he was a killer.

One day, a boy went for a walk at night but he didn't realise he was being followed.

A few seconds later, the gingerbread man crossed wolf jumped and got the boy and ripped him to bits.

JAMIE BAKER (11)
St Bernard's Catholic High School, Barrow-in-Furness

PUMPKINS

She heard the clock strike twelve. She dashed away to the carriage only to find it a pumpkin. She set out sprinting again, as fast as she could go, every step wearing her down, step… step… step… step… She fell to her knees and heard a growl behind her. She turned. She focused, a wolf! In desperation she scrambled up a tree. The wolf followed…

SCARLETT KENNY (11)
St Bernard's Catholic High School, Barrow-in-Furness

An Apple A Day Keeps The Prince Away

There in the woods… a coffin! There lay Little Miss Fairest. Seven grieving men. A prince came along. A smooch on the lips and bang, he was gone. He lay on the floor with death in his eyes. Tiny Snow White had a surprise. A small little apple was on her lips. She then dropped dead. The toxin there, apple red on her lips. Seven small dwarfs and two dead bodies. I wonder how this will look?

Lucas Kay (12)
St Bernard's Catholic High School, Barrow-in-Furness

Gingerbread Jack

The giant heard it. That irritable noise from his past - Jack's giggle. The incorrigible rascal had once before disturbed his peace and now he was back to steal his golden crown. 'You'll not escape this time,' the giant bellowed. Locking the door tightly, he thudded around the room and searched thoroughly for Jack but couldn't see him anywhere. Now Jack jumped from the frying pan and into the fire. Upon hearing the giant's call he hid in what he believed to be a cupboard, but it was an oven. When the giant discovered Jack he decided to bake Gingerbread Jack.

Charlotte North (11)
St Bernard's Catholic High School, Barrow-in-Furness

THE GLOWING TREE

He screamed with fear as a strange-looking wolf came towards him. It had red eyes, pointy teeth and grey fur. We never backed off, we stayed strong like men. 'Deano,' Sid shouted. 'He's got my arm, get off me!' Deano got a sharp, pointy stick off the twisted tree. Deano tried to get the wolf by the neck and tried to kill it. At least it got off his arm. We found a note saying: 'To defeat the wolf - push a button on the glowing tree'. They found the glowing tree, that was the last of the wolf.

JOSEPH THOMPSON (13)
St Bernard's Catholic High School, Barrow-in-Furness

FINDING THE INNER BEAST

There she stood. All was silent. All was calm. Taking a few steps closer, she dwelled upon her daunting experiences that shone before her very eyes. Out of all the trauma she'd endured, this was the one that triggered the bullet in her brain. It couldn't be, could it? She took one, just one, little step closer, her shaky hands beginning to touch for the first time. There was nothing there. She didn't understand! There was something, there had to be! She fell to the floor, gradually breaking down. Tears poured. Yelps broke out. She was the demon.

BETHANY HEWSON (11)
St Bernard's Catholic High School, Barrow-in-Furness

THE QUEST

As the knight galloped on his noble steed approaching the ferocious dragon, he tingled out of his shining armour that glistened as bright as the moon. Suddenly, he stabbed the petrifying beast and whipped the thorny trees as something black as raven rose like fire from Hell that was blazing up to Heaven. Soon the brave knight swung his sword while the thorns dug into his eyes, leaving it blind, and leaving him with scars of victory. He stumbled off his steed and climbed the gigantic tower knowing that he would awaken a fair maiden to find a foul goblin!

VARENKA BRIGGS (11)
St Bernard's Catholic High School, Barrow-in-Furness

THE RESCUE

The door creaked. Hope. Her eyelids fluttered with desperation of stealing a short, sweet glance of her saviour. Years of painful patience had taken their toll. Her skin had crinkled and folded like an old letter. Her hair had grown wiry and grey; no longer christened with a tiara, now just dotted with dust. Footsteps shuffled closer, viciously slow. Beads of sweat dampened her frail shaking hands. His skin brushed against her. Her eyes opened. She grasped a cold knife and sank it into the flesh of the devoted man that hoped to save her. Patience isn't always a virtue.

LAUREN JEFFRIES (15)
Stratford-upon-Avon School, Stratford-upon-Avon

UNTITLED

The fairy godmother waved her glistening wand in small elegant circles and said her magical words. The pumpkin disappeared and right in front of my eyes and out of thin air, appeared a carriage - but not any normal carriage, a shining, golden carriage, coated in glitter. The fairy godmother stepped back and gave me a gentle nudge to get in. I held up my dress and walked slowly into the carriage. Abruptly, the small wooden door shut. Suddenly, the glitter fell to the floor, all the intricate decorations smashed on the ground. The fairy godmother smirked in the window. Darkness.

HANA ADLER (15)
Stratford-upon-Avon School, Stratford-upon-Avon

RED IN THE WIND

The young girl in the red cloak ran through the woods trying to escape the spots of rain that fell. Slowly, she drew to a stop to catch her breath. *Snap*. Quickly, she looked around but saw nothing. *Snap*. A man slowly staggering towards her wielding an axe. 'Woodcutter, are you OK?' she questioned with a relieved sigh. He never answered, and just kept stalking towards her. Bringing his axe to the side he swung it violently. The young girl's red hood went fluttering into the wind, never to be seen again.

HOLLY SUMNERS (15)
Stratford-upon-Avon School, Stratford-upon-Avon

MIRROR, MIRROR ON THE WALL, WHO'S THE DEADLIEST ONE OF ALL?

Before the clock struck the late hour of ten, Snow White staggered through her front door under the weight of another's body. The disfigured corpse that was collapsed on her shoulders was laced in both blood and sweat. There was only a single glazed eye in which circled a bruised socket. The body slumped onto the ageing pile of the unfortunate in the corner of the kitchen. Taking a sharpened knife, Snow White cut at an older, more withered body of a vexatious huntsman she had long passed. His rotting body was then prepared to be devoured by the waiting seven dwarfs.

FREYA STIFF (16)
Stratford-upon-Avon School, Stratford-upon-Avon

THE DARK FOREST OF SNOW

Once upon a time, there was a girl called Snow White who went out for a walk in the forest and never came back. Snow White met a cute wolf that turned into a blood-eating, fierce wolf. Snow White tried to run but tripped down the deep, dark hill. The wolf chased after her trying to capture her and kill her to eat her for lunch, but Snow White escaped. The only thing is the wolf has the scent of Snow White, so the evil human-eating wolf can easily find the injured sprinting princess, Snow White.

JAZMIN LEA CARTWRIGHT (14)
Stratford-upon-Avon School, Stratford-upon-Avon

TINKABLACK

Once upon a time, there was a magical fairy. She had a bright green dress with leaves in her hair. Her hair was in a tight elegant bun. But she wasn't at all elegant. She captured Peter Pan in a derelict land and put him in a cage. He was only allowed out if him and Tinkabell had a happy ever after. Tinkabell wasn't what you thought, she was a trap herself. She turned everything dark black where she sprinkled her glitter. What happened to her? She wasn't that small innocent girl we all knew, anymore!

FREYA BARNETT (14)
Stratford-upon-Avon School, Stratford-upon-Avon

LITTLE RED RIDING WOLF

She walks with her blood-red cape dragging along like a blade dripping with blood. As she strolls through the dark forest she hears something, footsteps patting along the cold mud. So she follows the noise and with every step she makes it becomes colder. It's a wolf! He stops, he turns, he looks… he goes. The bloodthirsty girl runs ahead in the shadows. Then a hut, with snoring noise. As mysterious as it is, she enters. The noise is getting louder with every creak of the wooden floor, but then the wolf comes to eat the girl whole.

LEWIS NOBLE (12)
Stratford-upon-Avon School, Stratford-upon-Avon

VINEGAR AND BROWN PAPER

Cries echoed around the unearthly cave as the pitiful infant wept tears of treachery. It was only a game that masked something more sinister. The girl's heart blackened as her brother's death consumed her. Innocence was once her true virtue but it was of no matter now, here in the desolate cave with her kin now floating cracked and bleeding in the jaws of the open ocean. She couldn't bear to once again trek up the wraithful cliff and pass the stagnant well. Their race, their game turned to one of life and all for a pail of water.

LILY MCMEEKAN (15)
Stratford-upon-Avon School, Stratford-upon-Avon

THE VILLAINS

The villains were having a quiet day when they heard a noise from overhead. They ran out, and saw the police trying to find them. They had the ultimate laser gun. The helicopter circled overhead so they went back inside and it went away. They went to work; when they had finished they loaded the gigantic gun into the car and sped off. When they arrived they jumped out quickly and stormed the building. They had a massive pair of doors in the way. What were they going to do? How were they going to kill the prime minister now?

DANIEL GODEFROY (14)
Stratford-upon-Avon School, Stratford-upon-Avon

EVIL LITTLE PIGS

Once upon a time, three little pigs were creating chaos in the mysterious and isolated woods. How would the pigs build their needed house? Spontaneously, a kind-hearted wolf came along and built them a house made of straw. However, the ungrateful pigs blew the house down!

The next day, the wolf came back and realised the house was gone so he made another house using twigs. But once again, they blew the house down and demanded a better one. Then the wolf built them a house made of bricks so the pigs were happy and they lived happily ever after.

OLIVIA JOAN BAILEY (12)
Stratford-upon-Avon School, Stratford-upon-Avon

SOMETIMES LIFE'S HARD

His light fingers made me feel so innocuous. His voice made me feel like fairy dust inside. Now all those feelings have been shattered into needles of loneliness. He hasn't just hurt me with his feelings and actions, but Father as well. Whilst I lay innocent and broken, he watched my stepmother helplessly, his heart beckoning over to the evil lady. His head nodded in agreement and as if a spell had been put on him, he wandered over to her and their scared hearts joined together. As everyone thought he was the swooping hero, he was cruelly lying everywhere.

RUBY WADE (12)
Stratford-upon-Avon School, Stratford-upon-Avon

KILLER DWARFS

One day, there were three little pigs. All of the pigs had their own house - one made of twigs, one made of straw, one made of bricks. They always had to be aware of the dwarfs, the dwarfs were always looking for somewhere to live and if you didn't give them your house, they would eat you alive!
One day, the dwarfs were looking around for a new house, they came to the house made of twigs. They went inside and asked the pig if they could have his house, he said, 'No.' What happened? The dwarfs ate him alive!

KIERA KENNEDY (11)
Stratford-upon-Avon School, Stratford-upon-Avon

LITTLE RED RIDING HOOD

She was running as fast as the wind; her blood-red cape following behind her. She was screaming with all her might, 'Aaaargh.' Suddenly, a spear as sharp as a sword flew past her and nearly cut her gorgeous brown wavy locks. Snow White was racing towards her with a sharp and evil look in her eyes but before she could say, 'I'm coming for you Red,' a large hairy beast stood guard and snarled. Snow White looked into the eyes of the beast and let out a scream that could shatter a thousand windows.

THALIE COLETA-SIBLEY (12)
Stratford-upon-Avon School, Stratford-upon-Avon

The Little Devil

He took everything I ever cared for. The only thing that persuaded me to live. My voice. Now it's gone. My own father snatched it from me. Just because of poor Mother's death he doesn't understand. He doesn't know what it feels to have nothing but a voice to remind me of Mother. He has to die. There is nothing left to say. Revenge will settle me. I sneak to the kitchen. I take a knife. I can't speak. I can't tell him that I love him or that I hate him. I feel tears in my eyes. Goodbye, Father.

Molly Rose Flanagan (12)
Stratford-upon-Avon School, Stratford-upon-Avon

Liar, Liar

'What will we do with a liar?'
Pinocchio muttered, 'I don't know.' But he did know, as he said this his nose grew and grew five feet long.
'A whip on the back will do that kid good.' So that's what Pinocchio got, a whip from a cane as large as an elephant's ear. The carpenter asked if it hurt, again, Pinocchio lied, again he got another whip. Pinocchio couldn't stand it anymore. He got a saw and chopped off his nose. *Chop, chop, chop,* his nose was all gone. Pinocchio was a normal kid again and now he's free.

Hannah Jeffs (11)
Stratford-upon-Avon School, Stratford-upon-Avon

THE THREE LITTLE GANGSTERS

In 1932, New York was a changed city. The Statue of Liberty and the Empire State Building had a great impact on everyday life. Not to mention the notorious gangsters that hunted and killed in the streets. But nobody remembers the three biggest, most frightful gangsters that even Al Capone and Settimo Accardi were scared of. The LaBronx Triplets: Edgar, Otto and Rich were the most feared of all new Jersey. They would rob, steal and kill anything they could get their grimy hands on, legend has it that the downfall of Capone was due to the triplets robbing him.

LOUIS SOBRAL-KILMISTER (12)
Stratford-upon-Avon School, Stratford-upon-Avon

THE HARMONY OF WAR

Thick blood oozed down my back. Tainted by the hatred of every soul its owner had heartlessly torn out like it was nothing but an inconvenience. The job was done. All my life; the pain; heartbreak, had all paid off. As I walked out, through the mismatch of body parts ruthlessly sliced off at uneven angles, shrouding the floor, my feet picked up corpses' lost limbs. The dead battlefields grew more still as I found myself trudging out of the forsaken castle, filled with hatred. An aggressive peace devoured the castle and the sun seared my wounds as I jumped...

DANIEL MALONE (15)
Stratford-upon-Avon School, Stratford-upon-Avon

Hooded Monster

Her ruby-red coat shadowed the girl in the wind. Feet thumped the bloodstained ground angrily. The girl's thin body was changing, morphing into something - something big and hairy. Dagger-sharp teeth emerged from her young, pretty smile. She ran, quickly; towards the distant cottage, where her grandmother lived. *Knock, knock!* Her oversized hand banged against the faded door. 'Come in dear,' a kind, innocent voice beckoned. The room was quiet, apart from the squeaking floorboards that lay beneath. 'Why, you look different,' the old lady exclaimed, 'and what big teeth you have!' A loud noise. Silence.

Mathilda Ward (12)
Stratford-upon-Avon School, Stratford-upon-Avon

The Little Mermaid

The ice-cold sea splashed upon my pale face. The young mermaid held out her scaly, green hand. She was beautiful. Her eyes were as blue as the sea and her locks as gold as the sand in the morning. She smiled; her sharp teeth glistening in the light of the rising sun. A menacing glint flashed in her eye. Her cold outstretched hand firmly grasped hold of mine. I felt a surge of urgency rush through me. She let go of my hand and glided through the icy sea, like a knife through butter.
I had to follow her…

Ellie Rose Marshall (12)
Stratford-upon-Avon School, Stratford-upon-Avon

A WAR ZONE

Shocked at what was going on, the three little pigs stared in horror. All you could see in Sleeping Beauty's eyes was evil. Screaming. Shouting. Everywhere was hell. A blazing hot fire roared as it got bigger. The three little pigs were in danger of becoming bacon! Why would Sleeping Beauty do such an evil thing? It was a war zone! Dead bodies lay everywhere, some burnt, some stabbed. A stream of blood bolted down the steep hill. *Thump! Thump! Thump!* The trees were like the hands on a clock, but falling every second with the power of Sleeping Beauty.

ELLA WILSON (12)
Stratford-upon-Avon School, Stratford-upon-Avon

RAPUNZEL AND THE SECRET MAN! (PETER PAN)

I sat there, companionless, looking out into the clear sapphire sky, not knowing what was waiting to happen. My golden hair swooped down to the soft grass which I'd never touched. As soon as I had the urge to escape, a figure flew past. I urgently perched right out the window but a little bit too far, my hair had already lumped up at the ground. I found myself in mid-air, my eyes were shut tight and I didn't want to open them. Sparkling and glistening in the light his eyes were glancing at mine. Who was he?

GEORGIE BURTON (12)
Stratford-upon-Avon School, Stratford-upon-Avon

Well, Well, Well

'Well, what do we have here boys. Snow? Where's your prince to save you? Oh yes, I forgot, you don't have one,' chuckled the seven dwarfs.
'Go away, I'm warning you!'
'Did you just threaten me? Take her away boys!'
The dwarfs started to creep up on Snow from all directions.
Slowly, Snow raised the apple she was holding firmly, 'I warned you,' she said in a sly voice. Violently, Snow threw her ruby-red apple onto the leaf-smothered green ground. Gas exploded everywhere and the dwarfs fell to the ground, unconscious. 'Who shall I eat first?' questioned Snow.

Nadia-Jane Rogers (12)
Stratford-upon-Avon School, Stratford-upon-Avon

Peter In A Pan

The crisp leaves shattered under Peter's feet as he chased his shadow through the dark sinister trees. In an instant, his shadow disappeared into a dark winding hole; with no hesitation, Peter foolishly followed. He landed in a dark room, lit by only a glow emitting from a small fire. Around the fire lay three pigs. One, distinctly different from the others, noticed him and oinked. 'Boys, wake up, fresh meat!'
The two other pigs rose and the three of them tied him up, bound him to a pole then hung him over the fire to roast, screaming in pain...

Joshua Stephens (12)
Stratford-upon-Avon School, Stratford-upon-Avon

GOLDY AND THE THREE MURDERS

Suddenly, she creepily stepped into the beaten cottage. Her murderous plan had succeeded. The three bears had no idea that sly Goldy was going to take their lives. She slowly sauntered across the floorboards and spotted the furry species gobbling their steaming, bubbling porridge. It was crunch time. Hair standing, dress flowing and blood revealing, a risky jump scared the three bears out of their wooden chairs. 'Argh!' they cried. 'What has brought you here?' 'Death has brought me here,' Goldy slurred. She tugged out a shining blade and one by one, like a knife in butter, sliced their furry throats.

EDIE CLARKE (12)
Stratford-upon-Avon School, Stratford-upon-Avon

STRINGS

It was just meant to be a game; we always played games. The strings were sewn in with such dexterity, it would be fraudulent to deny the allure. His eyes were a spellbinding green, it was wondrous to see the pure fear reflected in them, they looked exceptional in the glass jar. It was a magnificent mess, my thirst was quenched. He always spoke of how one day I would obtain a heartbeat: perhaps now I could have his. Serenity, I pulled the strings, the arms moved in sync, my heart sang in euphoria, I was a real boy.

HANNAH HILLIER (15)
Stratford-upon-Avon School, Stratford-upon-Avon

Short Stories

What no one tells you about fairy tales is what happens after...
The pigs lived together in their own brick house. But there was one problem: The wolf's big bad brother had found out where they lived and was hunting them. The wolf had an axe and chopped down a tree, he then blocked the pigs in so there was no escape. He waited outside until they resorted to cannibalism. Finally, when there was only one pig left he entered the house with his axe. With one swipe, he sliced his head off. He had his revenge!

William Jones (12)
Stratford-upon-Avon School, Stratford-upon-Avon

Black Death

Sat at home alone. Waiting for the unknown. Hearing that familiar tune. Waiting for the near future to loom. Teeth gnashing. Fists bashing. Voices like gravel. As they go on their travel, the green fleshy toxic sphere, it creates an evil, eerie, uneasy atmosphere. The burning bite. Blockaded the light. Along came Prince Charming. To save me from the harming. But nobody knows what the future can hold. To the Devil my life I sold. Death comes with a kiss. This world I'll truly miss. He went down with a thud. Lying in a pool of his own crimson blood.

Bethany Caitlin Harris (15)
Stratford-upon-Avon School, Stratford-upon-Avon

MOVEMENT

Maybe it was a dream. A horror story I had read earlier in life. But the problem was, I could not wake up. I knew it was a dream. Perhaps they were right. I was going crazy. Why didn't I leave right now? The door was right open. Probably some sort of test. I couldn't move. I felt like stone. I could move my arms and hands, just not my legs and feet. I fumbled around in my pocket. I brought out a mirror. Half of my face had been ripped off and I could see my jaw and eyeball...

TERI ANN CHADWICK (12)
Ullswater Community College, Penrith

TILL DEATH DO US PART

The girl gulped with fear, wondering what torture she would go through today, what food would be viciously shoved down her throat. 'Is it sheep's salty brains or sugary scorpions and salty spiders?' She was knocked out for ten minutes, forced into a dark crumbling building, tied up with rope. A mystical creature storming through the building with an army of mutant rats, stealing children to do their bidding. She was brutally beaten up with a baseball bat. She plotted her revenge. She had to kill... She had to escape but what about the death traps? She will eventually escape...

GABRIELLE JANE BAILEY (12)
Ullswater Community College, Penrith

UNTITLED

The girls were sleeping. The trees were whistling. The stream was singing. It was coming. The sound of the galloping hooves, still it rings in my head and the screams of my friends still torture me. The tents have gone, my friends have gone. The crackling fire and the loud footsteps. The howl of the wolf and black blanket of sadness. It's coming, it's coming. The midnight blackness haunting. The loud wind blows. It's coming, it's coming. It's getting louder, it's getting louder. Will it stop, will it stop? Make it stop, make it stop. It's now here...

DAVINA LOUISE IVINSON MCANENEY (12)
Ullswater Community College, Penrith

THE MISSING DWARF!

I was wandering through the woods, singing to the birds while collecting wild berries for my seven friends, Doc, Grumpy, Happy, Sleepy, Bashful, Sneezy and Dopey. When I finally got back to the village it was hectic! Sneezy came over to me, sneezing between every word that came out of his tiny little mouth. He panicked and sneezed... and sneezed again. 'Dopey! Achoo, he, achoo, he's gone!' he spluttered. Grumpy looked like a bomb, ready to explode, he had musky steam coming out of his ears, his eyes glaring at me, I was about to scream... I turned around...

LAUREN HANNAH CLARKE (12)
Ullswater Community College, Penrith

DARKNESS

She learnt to live off the land. Hunting. Scavenging the forest for food. The animals in the forest knew she was in charge but then everything changed. The world went dark. As she lifted her head to see what had happened, a face loomed over her, sharp teeth dripping with blood, long snout, mouth foaming, but the most hideous thing was the eyes: amber, piercing like they had seen everything. He was a wolf on her territory. He was a lot bigger than her so she ran. As she ran she wasn't careful. She ran into a tree. It went dark...

EVIE FARNDON (12)
Ullswater Community College, Penrith

THE WOLF

I saw him - the wolf - his grey coat shining in the moonlight. This hunter was about to become the hunted. He saw me; my blood-red cloak had given me away. But soon I would have a new cloak made of wolf fur. I pulled out my knife but he saw me again and this time he fled, running like the wind through the emerald-green forest.
The wolf looked back, his yellow eyes glowing. In the blink of an eye, he was gone. My chance was gone. I slowly walked away.
He wasn't coming back.
The lone grey wolf.

ROSIE ELIZABETH DALE (12)
Ullswater Community College, Penrith

THE GIRL

The girl smiled. She was finally big enough to cut through the woods. Oranges, greens and browns hid from her bright red coat. As she went deeper into the woods the trees thickened, the sky grew dark, it got colder until the girl was huddled inside her thin, red coat. That's when she heard it. The ghostly howl that went right through her. Then she saw it. The ghastly girl covered in blood. She beckoned. The girl screamed, turned and ran. But she stopped, she thought she felt a hand on her shoulder. She turned, it was the ghastly girl...

FREYA COLLING (12)
Ullswater Community College, Penrith

DISGUSTING RICHES

I could have anything, whatever I wanted. They were in their dining room. 'Just go ask,' I said. My sister was still too afraid though. They were playing Russian roulette (so I knew why my sister didn't want to go in there). Then suddenly, there was a crash as my dad fell to the floor. A deafening scream came from my mum, she never wanted to play, she was too afraid. It was my uncle, he convinced him, just for his kicks, what a grimy man. This was the story of my horrible, disgusting, destructive, low-hearted life...

DANIEL BENNETT (12)
Ullswater Community College, Penrith

THE REFLECTION

As I walked towards the old ancient door, I could hear the wind whispering in my left ear. It gave me a shiver of coldness. Shivering, I could feel the wind biting at my face. The door. It opened by itself! I stood on something. It was a mat. The mat said: 'Rellik'. A light turned on. Above me was a mirror. Something dripped on me. It was bright red. Blood! I looked in the mirror again. The reflection of the mat said: 'Killer'. I was scared. I shouted for help. There was a reply. Was I alone?

LAYLA THRELKELD (12)
Ullswater Community College, Penrith

THE CREATURE

There I stood. Feeling his warm breath brush past my wet face. It happened so fast. First my sister, with tears running down her face. Then my brother whose face was red from the creature's crushing hands, but all I could hear was silence. I hid with my soft cover pushed up against my face. I heard my parents talking about recent disappearances, but then they stopped and then I heard them spring up the stairs. When they came up they were in for a surprise.

SAMUEL POTTS (12)
Ullswater Community College, Penrith

THE GHOSTLY GIRL

On top of the misty mountains sits a haunted castle, full of dull, narrow corridors. It has been haunted for many years now. No one dares go there. People who go there are never to be seen again. It's haunted by a young girl - Annie she was called. The last time she was seen, she was sat on a high wall next to a river at the bottom of the misty mountains surrounded by tall glowing trees. She decided to go and explore the mountain tops. She shouldn't have. She climbed to the top to find the creepy, haunted castle...

EMILY LAW (12)
Ullswater Community College, Penrith

THE GIANT SNATCHERS - BFG

In the middle of the night when the stars are out, all the children are snuggled up in bed. Sleeping sweet dreams. Little did they know that the strange big hands would creep through the window to snatch them away. Windows now had nobody behind them with the horrified parents unknown where they are. With the giants eating away on the innocent children (who didn't think this would happen on this night). Yum, yum! Distant sobs and screams from the children's parents. The giants walked away back home satisfied as can be. Something had to be done! The BFG.

LILY WEBB (11)
Ullswater Community College, Penrith

THE TEACHER OF 'MAGIC'

There was once a boy. But this boy was different. He received an anonymous letter. It told him to go to the mysterious building hidden deep in the valley. He accepted, not aware of the danger he was putting himself in. The building was dull and he met another unaware, innocent child. It was a 'school', and their first 'lesson' was shape-shifting. They didn't know of the consequences. During his shape-shift, he was pushed, and only half of him appeared. It was as if he was ripped apart slowly, as he was in the space between life and death...

EDWARD SPENCE (12)
Ullswater Community College, Penrith

THE BFG'S HAND

Children are sleeping. Not knowing who's next. Just after nightfall the windows might be locked but nothing stops them. They come, ready to snatch them. Then the hand goes through the window. Before you can move, you are trapped. Many try and fail to retaliate. The window's left open and the bed empty. At daybreak all over town parents are crying. There are many reports to the police of children being snatched out of their homes, and there is nothing anyone can do. But there is one good giant who blows good dreams into children's ears, called the BFG.

JAKE STAMPER (12)
Ullswater Community College, Penrith

THE FOREST

She stood there. Who was she? I'd heard about this forest, was it true? I stepped back; the leaves crackled as I moved. Did she hear me? It was silent. I heard that a demon ruled these woods, wandering, looking for her next victim. Could I be next? The fear was taking over me, I couldn't control myself. I stepped forward, my heart was beating so loud I bet she could hear me. Another step. *Boom, boom!* My heart wouldn't stop pounding. A slight moment could change everything. What should I do? I felt sick. What if I was wrong?

ELLIE HOWARD (12)
Ullswater Community College, Penrith

THE HAUNTED HOUSE

Just on the horizon. There it is. The house I've been sent to. Amongst the fog. Where I can't see. Crows are cawing, beckoning me. The dull doorknob squeals in protest. It's a warning. Warning to stay away. The door slams shut behind. I'm in a haunted house! My breath starts to quicken. My heartbeat rises, I hear small whispers beckoning me in. The whispers are louder as I near the lounge. Hesitating, I lean against a drawer. The years of dust blow away at my touch. I open the door, it squeals in protest. Then just plain nothingness.

KATIE JACKSON (12)
Ullswater Community College, Penrith

THE EMERALD CITY...

It was the emerald city. The city was emerald. I had heard tales of this place. My ruby-red slippers were starting to hurt. I needed to look for a place to sit down. I walked past the glistening pool, I heard a splash. Before I knew it, I was in the pool, sinking deep down inside the earth. I rubbed my eyes and looked around. A tin man, a scarecrow and a lion singing songs! They suddenly turned and all charged at me with hacksaws! Sparkles in their eyes. They'd cut off each limb before I could scream a word...

MACY ELLA HICKS (12)
Ullswater Community College, Penrith

WHERE DOES THE QUEEN LIVE?

Falling into dusk; the night sky was an inky black sea. With joyous emerald-green lights, the mood was lit up. Magically glistening like angelic angels elegantly dancing in the sky, the stars shone brightly. Beyond the golden tranquil lake led a flight of magnificent stairs, which revealed the majestic, precious palace. As the tall trees shook their dusty winter coats, Sophia stood awestruck at the grand gates of the palace. Calmly, she gathered her nerves and stepped into the palace courts, to seek the queen's permission to enter the neighbouring country... Her access had been granted: She was relieved!

NAOMI HARRIS (12)
Ullswater Community College, Penrith

Return Of The Giants

The night was cold, very cold - in fact it was almost snowing.
Suddenly, out of the darkness came three large blue, hairy and
disgusting figures. The ground shook as they walked, the lights
dimmed and two cats, Whiskers and Jim, stopped fighting and ran
indoors.
'They're back,' said an old man. 'Giants are back,' he said, while
sneakily peeking out his window.
Very suddenly the air warmed up and parents of children opened
their bedroom windows to keep them asleep.
That was a big mistake.
When the sun arose, terrified screams of parents filled the valley... all
the children, gone.

JAMIE COWPERTHWAITE (11)
Ullswater Community College, Penrith

THE LOST GHOST

There was a hurricane, windows were wide open, banging, curtains and bed sheets were flying. She went downstairs, nobody was home and she got worried. Her phone was ringing but she missed the calls. However, she tried to ring them and she ended up being outside because of 'no signal'. Unfortunately, she couldn't ring them back. The door creaked and *bang!* She got locked outside. She was shaking in fear and coldness, she walked to ask for help until she found herself in the woods. She got hit by the thunder and died. The lost ghost's body was not found.

BEAH LAMIS (12)
Ullswater Community College, Penrith

OFF TRACK

The tall trees stand. The little girl in a red cloak expects nothing as she begins her journey. The sunlight peers through the trees. She hears a rustle nearby. It's just the wind, or is it? She stands still. A shadow starts moving towards her. She slowly starts to walk off the track, away from the shadow. The sun appears over the trees. She looks. She's lost. She doesn't know where to go or what to do. Then the stumbling shadow is there again, this time she waits for it. It appears to only be an old man wanting directions.

CHARLOTTE CARRICK (12)
Ullswater Community College, Penrith

THE CREATURE IN THE WOODS

She stands there. Who is she? I've heard about these woods, is it true? I step back, leaves cracking. Did she hear me? I have a churning lump in my throat but I'm too afraid to swallow just in case she hears the fright in my breath... Why isn't she scared of me? She isn't like the others! I wonder if there's more like her? Will they come and get me?
Just one step closer and I feel my heart stop! There is no sign of fright? What is she going to do to me? I'm scared!

CHLOE DALTON (13)
Ullswater Community College, Penrith

SNATCHING

Silently creeping in and out of houses. In-between offices, looking
through each window, choosing. 'Which one? Not him, or her.'
Parents normally want children to go to bed early. Not in this town.
'Argh!' you hear, 'My baby!'
You run to the window, only to see a mother sobbing her heart out at
the window and a silhouette running down the road. You never see
the person. Only the silhouette, a giant maybe? He or she is as tall as
a block of flats. Their hand is massive. I am very surprised that it fits
through the small window.

MOLLY ELLA KIRKMAN (12)
Ullswater Community College, Penrith

LITTLE RED'S TWIST!

One day, I was wandering through the woods, but I felt like someone
was watching me. I told myself it was nothing. I was looking around,
trying to find the path underneath the overgrown grass. I found it.
But as I was going to Granny's house, a wolf jumped in front of me
and said, 'I want to eat you!' I was scared but then I remembered
what Granny said, 'Run into a wolf, batter him!' So that's what I did, I
battered the wolf. Then I skipped to Granny's house in a bloodstained
dress and a wolf skin hat.

SHANNON SOUTHWARD (12)
Ullswater Community College, Penrith

NIGHTFALL

Nightfall. They're coming, you can hear the growl of their breath, the screams of parents as they find the empty beds of their children, you can see the shadows ripple across the curtains with a sack slung over their back like a robber running away with a bag of money. With axe in hand, they spread into people's houses and grab the kids, throw them in the sack and run off into the night, everyone thinking, *will I be next?* People have started to fight back these creatures of the night but can they hold them back? Will they lose?

ROBERT HOPKINSON (11)
Ullswater Community College, Penrith

THE IVY INCIDENT

There's an uneasiness that remains as you're walking in the same forest that your best friend died in.
As I took each cautious step deeper into the woods it didn't take long to realise that I was lost. I searched for a path looking everywhere. Then I heard it.
It started to slither towards me, it wrapped around my leg and dragged me to the floor. As I realised this was how my friend had died, I struggled for freedom, but this only made it worse. I was dragged towards a big hole. Then in the hole I saw death...

ISABELLA GRACE NATTRASS (12)
Ullswater Community College, Penrith

THE KNIVES

One misty night, Little Black Riding Hood set off on the death trip of her life. Little Black Riding Hood came across six white ninjas the same night right outside her leader's cabin. The six white ninjas took her back to their base on the outskirts of the forest, not knowing that she had 12 black knives in her pockets. She cut the ropes and killed all six ninjas; she had just got the leader to kill. What she did not know was that her leader had betrayed her for the white army. The fight began.

ALEX HUDDART (12)
Ullswater Community College, Penrith

'NEVER LOOK BACK'

JayJay was leaving his mum's grave late at night. She died when he was four.
As he was walking, he passed his old school. As he carried on walking, he felt arms wrap around him almost like he was getting a hug. He couldn't move as the grasping kept a tight hold. He turned around, there his mum stood with a face ripped to shreds. As she yelled, 'JayJay!' he ran for his life. Before JayJay died of old age he gave you a message, to remember never ever look back. Because for all you know, anything could be behind!

NIAMH BRENAN (11)
Ullswater Community College, Penrith

UNTITLED

'Charlie! Run down for some tea, would you?'
Wearily, the small boy put on his shoes and buttoned up his coat. His
mum always wanted him to do the shopping.
On his way, an ancient man gave him some money. 'Go and buy
me a beer and keep the rest.' With the change, Charlie bought five
chocolate bars and one of them had nothing inside but the rest had
£9,000,000 inside as well as the chocolate!
He ran as fast as possible back home and his mum said, 'We are
going to be rich!'
'No, it's all mine,' said Charlie.

SAVANNAH EDWARDS-LYNCH (12)
Ullswater Community College, Penrith

THE ORPHANAGE

I approached the village at dusk. It was silent. There was me and me
only. The air was damp and the road was cobbled. A black cat with
green glary eyes stared at me then it pranced over the wall. There
it was. The tall, black, stone, creepy orphanage. I hate them, I hate
them with a passion. I wandered slowly up the hill as the orphanage
grew bolder and taller. The gates were iron with points as sharp as
daggers on top. I walked to the huge door. It opened. I said, 'You've
murdered my sister, you vile vulture!'

SASKIA TODD (12)
Ullswater Community College, Penrith

LITTLE RED RIDING HOOD

All she hears is the birds chirping and leaves rustling, she is singing and humming her favourite nursery rhymes with a basket in hand, she comes to a stop. She hears a strange sound, it sounds like a wolf. The tension is building, the sound is getting closer and closer. She has nowhere to run, she stands her ground. She sees a shadow passing tree to tree, turning small then big. There is now a growling and snorting noise. She exclaims, 'Who's there?'
The figure replies, 'Why are you here?'
She is afraid to reply back. Green eyes appear...

CHARLIE KIRKLAND (12)
Ullswater Community College, Penrith

DON'T GROW UP: IT'S A TRAP

Wendy let out a suffocating gasp. Were her eyes deceiving her? No... This was no trick from her mind. She watched in horror as Peter Pan brutally slaughtered her younger brothers, yelling, 'You're growing up!' The young female started to back away but to her surprise, she slammed straight into someone's chest... Captain Hook. The captain placed his hook against her shoulder and spoke with a hushed tone. 'Hush... I too used to be a Lost Boy... ' Hook whispered. 'I ran away before I too suffered the same fate from growing up.'

KELINA MAY MARSHALL (14)
William Howard School, Brampton

AWAKENING?

He had heard this story before; the princess lay unmoving on the bed before him. All he had to do was kiss her to awaken her from her deep slumber. The prince moved closer and kissed her ruby-red lips. No reaction. She was as still as ever, no fluttering eyelids, no intake of breath. It was then he realised she was lifeless, nothing more than a decaying corpse left untouched for one hundred years. The princess was dead.

CHARLOTTE HETHERINGTON (14)
William Howard School, Brampton

GREASY

Once upon a time, there was a young maiden locked away in a tower with extra long golden hair. As she was locked in a tower, she had no shower resources and as the years went on her hair became longer and greasier by the day.
One day, a young prince found himself outside the maiden's tower. He yelled, 'Rapunzel, let down your hair.' As she chucked down her long golden locks of greasy hair, he began to climb it. When he reached the top he slipped and fell to his death, pulling Rapunzel with him. There's no happy ending.

LEWIS LOGIE (14)
William Howard School, Brampton

ALICE IN HER LAND

They were waiting. Alice was now talking about a disappearing cat that could talk. 'A Cheshire cat I think.' She was laughing hysterically. 'And here he is now! Afternoon Mr Pussy Cat! This is my family and my doctor! Ha ha ha!' More laughter from Alice. As she said goodbye to her cat, Alice's parents, teary eyed, exchanged looks with the doctor. A look that said everything the doctor needed to know. Pulling out the toxic encrypted blanket, the doctor spoke, 'Hold still Alice. You'll be in your wonderland very soon.' It was Alice's last memory of the asylum.

EMILY GARSON (14)
William Howard School, Brampton

YOUNG WRITERS INFORMATION

We hope you have enjoyed reading this book – and that you will continue to in the coming years.

If you're a young writer who enjoys reading and creative writing, or the parent of an enthusiastic poet or story writer, do visit our website www.youngwriters.co.uk. Here you will find free competitions, workshops and games, as well as recommended reads, a poetry glossary and our blog.

If you would like to order further copies of this book, or any of our other titles give us a call or visit **www.youngwriters.co.uk**.

Young Writers
Remus House
Coltsfoot Drive
Peterborough
PE2 9BF

(01733) 890066 / 898110
info@youngwriters.co.uk